I0521265

DEAD LIKE ROMI

BOOK 3 IN THE LYNCH BROTHERS SERIES

HEATHER NOVAK

ALSO BY HEATHER NOVAK

EDIE'S AUTOMOTIVE GUIDE SERIES:

Headlights, Dipsticks, & My Ex's Brother

Fire Trucks, Garter Belts, & My Perfect Ex

Backseats, Spreadsheets, & My New Neighbor (Coming Soon)

THE LYNCH BROTHERS SERIES

Hunting Witch Hazel

Threat of Raine

To Amber Young, without whom I would have let this book rot in hell. Even after losing every single copy in a weird corrupted-haunted-file-of-doom-and-electronic-destruction, she wouldn't let me give up. You are the wind beneath its pages and all that.

To my siblings, I know I'm everyone's favorite, but you're all MY favorite.

To Shelly Bell, Aliza Mann, Sage Spelling, & MK Schiller who started this journey with me.

(Also, to Lucifer, because have you seen Tom Ellis shirtless?)

And, as always, in loving memory of my mom

Xoxo, H

SERIES NOTE

Dead Like Romi is the third and final book in The Lynch Brothers Trilogy. Books one and two—*Hunting Witch Hazel* and *Threat of Raine*—can be read as standalones, however, *Dead Like Romi* cannot. It is highly recommended that to fully experience Romi's and Fenton's stories and character arcs, that you start at *Hunting Witch Hazel*.

If you choose not to read books one and two first, or if you need a refresher, here are the important players:

Hazel Evanora: Witch, excellent bartender, and manager of Billy's Blues and BBQ, the only bar with live music in town. She started to sell off her power to pay off her parents' dark magic debt, but once her parents were incarcerated, she was able to regain full power.

Rosemary "Romi" Evanora: Hazel's twin sister who died at 18 in a car accident as a warning to their parents about their dark magic debt. Romi is a ghost tethered to Hazel's powers and has not crossed over into the afterlife. At the end of Threat of Raine, we learn that Romi is not the "average" ghost but is cursed.

Rune "Fenton" Lynch: Youngest Lynch brother, pacifist, kidnapped by Hazel's father. He and Romi are soulmates.

Baelfire "Grayson" Lynch: Middle Lynch brother and ex-witch hunter. Hasn't spoken to either of his brothers in the two years since their father died. Is tasked with trying to steal Hazel's powers as the ransom for Fenton's life when Fenton is kidnapped. He falls for Hazel during this mission and finds an alternative way to save both Fenton and Hazel, with the help of his friends and brother. He and Hazel are soulmates.

Lucian "Loren" Lynch: Eldest Lynch brother who works for an elite "hunting" organization, which tracks down abusers of magic and trafficking victims. He's called into Hayvenwood to help save his little brother. A demon with a grudge names Noiran follows and tries to destroy the town. Loren works with Galinda (a strong healing witch) and Javier (another hunter). He submitted his resignation at the end of Threat of Raine. He and Raine are soulmates.

Lorraine "Raine" Marche: A piano player at Billy's who is psychometric—she can tell the history of things and people with a single touch—and a gray witch, which is an incredibly powerful witch. She and Loren fell in love four years ago, when he was on a failed secret mission that left Raine's mother dead. She reconnects with Loren during the town's battle against the demon. Raine gives up her powers in order to kill Noiran and save the town. Raine's late mother (Genevieve) and the Lynch brothers' late mother (Laura) help her destroy the demon.

Pont d'Amor Bridge: Connects Hayvenwood University to off-campus housing. Hazel put a "love spell" on the bridge at the beginning of Hunting Witch Hazel for Romi's 21st birthday.

This book starts the day after the snowstorm in Threat of Raine, before the epilogue.

I hope you enjoy this final visit to Hayvenwood!

1

I had always envisioned death as the opposite of life—a permanent state of completely *gone,* instead of temporarily *here.* Everything had always fallen into these two, distinct categories: alive and dead. My first cat, my grandmother, our next-door neighbor, all here then gone in a single moment. There were no phantom whispers, no strange shadows in the mirrors, no visual hallucinations. There was a hard line, a one-way street, double doors with no re-entry between the worlds.

Except for me, apparently.

I remember when I died. The spectacular car crash, the circle of dark magic finally complete at the ripe old age of eighteen. A life for a life, with a two-year grace period. I always thought I could outrun the debt, that maybe mom would help me instead of being in denial—I know, how naive of me—that somehow I'd find a loophole. I had brought my father back from the dead, but he was no longer the man who had taught me to make peanut butter cookies or paint a wall. He was something much more sinister; a soul decaying while his body lived.

My last heartbeat still haunted me. It was barely a twinge, a small and insignificant thing scientifically, but the worst thing in the world for the people who loved me. Especially for my twin sister, Hazel, who held my hand as the curse took everything from her: our parents, me, and last remnants of her safety.

Mom went crazy after Dad disappeared with his new life, and then off the rails when I died. Hazel was the one who paid the price then, too. She was stalked by the assholes to whom our parents owed money, plagued by PTSD from the accident, kidnapped, roughed up by a demon, and the bar she managed was nearly destroyed by an apocalyptic snow storm.

All because of one can of bread crumbs. All because of me. At least there was one thing I could do for her, even though I was little more than a haunting. I could kick some serious demon ass.

The snow storm and bastard demon Noiran's demise had only occurred twenty-four hours ago, yet more demons were already daring to come back around to look for trouble. I was happy to give it to them. My arms wrapped around the middle-aged man's neck, who was currently being used as a spacesuit by a real asshole of a demon named Hysin. Hysin was unlikely to leave human flesh in proper working order when he was through with them, but it was a good thing I wasn't strong enough to crush this human's windpipe. Being a spirit had its advantages, like not getting hurt during a demon attack.

With a roar, I ripped Hysin out of the man, tossing them in opposite directions. The demon had killed two pets this week and I was done with his bullshit. The shadow form of the demon, more smoke-like than solid, curled in on itself in shock and then straightened out when it noticed me.

"Fuck you Evanora!" Hysin said, in every language, yet without making an audible sound. "That one was tasty."

"Gross." I circled him, watching for the telltale sign of his next move. Demons were fast, but they weren't seamless like spirits. Their edges were messy and left trails in the air. Each movement was practically outlined ahead of time.

Left hook, right kick, circle. Accepted a punch, but returned three more. Then, Hysin made a crucial error and let me get on his back. Did he not learn his lesson literally minutes ago?

"I keep sending you back to Hell, yet you keep returning. I really need to talk to someone in management down there," I teased. When I finished with a demon, they usually disappeared for a few months, but this one was becoming a weekly occurrence. I would've been worried, but he sucked at fighting.

Hysin laughed a gnarled, twisted sound. "You may have escaped Hell once, Evanora, but you won't escape a second time. Soon, you'll be down there with me."

I rolled my eyes. "All I hear is blah blah blah, I got my ass kicked by a girl, blah blah." It probably wasn't a good idea to taunt demons, but I was my sister's twin, and honestly, our sarcasm was genetic.

"Next time, I'm coming back for you!" the demon threatened.

"Over my dead body," my boyfriend Fenton—is that really the right word for a living-ghost pairing?—called, stepping into the alley we had turned into a boxing ring holding a small, wooden box.

I *tsked*. "Oh, you shouldn't have done that. Now you've made him mad."

Fenton flipped open the box and started chanting. Hysin tried to wrestle out of my grasp, pleading, but he was already being pulled into what we called Pandora's box. If I was alive, it would be super dangerous for me to be anywhere near the innocuous wood, which was originally a witch hunting tool used to collect the powers and souls of witches. I figured out that if I recalibrated the box just right —adding a symbol on the side with a sharp knife—it would trap a demon. I didn't know how long it would take them to weasel their way out of the box yet, this was only a test run. I hoped it was a few millennia.

Look, it wasn't my fault that I had overheard Javier and Galinda, coworkers of my boyfriend's brother who were badass monster hunters, talk about the different potential uses for the box. And if I happened to go through a laptop that was left open, well accidents happened. I'd happily give them credit for the research, but I was ready to take it all the way to the testing stages before they were. Haunting people was always a toss up; sometimes I saw hairy butts, sometimes I discovered really useful information.

I leaned down close to Hysin. "You better get a last look around, asshole, because you're about to be the genie in the lamp."

"Romi!" My boyfriend—soulmate? partner? *mon chéri*? *petit ami*?—called, and I let go of the demon as the rest of him was sucked inside. Fenton snapped the lid closed and flipped the latch. "Good job, babe. I'll need to order more boxes. We only have one left." He pursed his lips and I kissed him. Well, put pressure on his mouth. I couldn't actually feel his lips, just warmth where they touched me.

The innocuous-looking box was no bigger than a large encyclopedia volume, but it was like a black-hole. Keeping it firmly tucked under his arm, he ran over to the human-suit the demon was using and checked for a pulse. By the expletive that fell from his mouth, I knew we were too late.

Fenton left him resting in the remnants of the apocalyptic snow storm that had blown through town yesterday.

I wrapped my arm—well, tried to—around his lower back. "If it makes you feel any better, we can bury Hysin in consecrated ground if it's not too frozen. Really piss him off."

He shrugged. "Yeah, a little. Let me text Javier so he can call in the victim. Then I'll grab the shovel."

I leaned up and pressed a kiss to his cheek. "Meet you back at the hotel."

I stopped using his energy and faded back through the veil and into the in-between, a world crushed between the living and dead. A place where I wasn't meant to exist. It was supposed to be the transitional space for spirits on their way to the afterlife.

I had seen shimmers and shadows pass through, but they never stayed. Never talked to me, never acknowledged that they knew I was there. I was totally and completely alone.

2

Before I could even tie my own shoes, I dedicated my life to pacifism. I didn't want to hunt witches, despite being the descendant of generations of hunters. I got the family's gray cross tattoo across my shoulder blade on my eighteenth birthday three years ago, but to me, it symbolized the bond with my brothers, not that I was a hunter.

There was already too much hate in the world, especially over things people had no control over. You couldn't control if you were born a witch any more than you could control being born a witch hunter. I wasn't in the habit of disliking people because of things they couldn't control. I didn't hunt witches, people, or animals, and was a proud vegan by age five.

Hunting demons with Romi, however, was the rush I never knew I needed. The kind that filled my nights with more than just cheap booze and reruns with laugh tracks. To be honest, she was doing all the hunting and I was trapping. The ancient itch buried deep inside me was mollified, and in the process, I was protecting innocent people.

When I walked into my motel room after disposing of Hysin, I was ready for dinner and lounging around with my pants off. I knew as soon as the sun came up, we'd have to deal with the aftermath of the snow storm and I was exhausted. The snow, for the most part, had officially melted by sunset tonight, leaving behind mostly minor damage and a lot of ice.

I kicked off my shoes and put the shovel away in the closet. Room number six at the Hayvenwood Motel was seriously old two decades ago and there were a few stains on the carpet I vowed not to examine too closely, but it was still cozy with a really strong heater.

A prickling sensation ran over my skin, a warning that Romi was nearby, and I smiled. "The ground is almost completely frozen, so we need to find a new place to put the boxes," I told her. "But got him buried right under and angel statue and—*holy hell* you're not my girlfriend!" I dropped my backpack and bent over double at the waist, trying to catch my breath.

"Nope. Definitely not," my older brother, Loren, said. He sat on the unused second double bed, flipping through television stations. "I like how this place doesn't have cable. That's how you know it's vintage."

I motioned with my hand. "A text was too impersonal? An email? It's only been..." I glanced at my watch, "twenty-four hours since you've seen me. Shouldn't you be home, taking care of your girlfriend?" I looked back at the hotel room door. "How'd you get in here anyway?"

He turned off the television. "You aren't happy to see me? I'm your favorite brother! Also, please don't insult me by asking how I got through a locked door. And Presley, Raine's roommate, is looking after her."

I rolled my eyes. "First off, I don't have a favorite brother.

You're both my favorite. Although Grayson's winning at the moment because he didn't just make me nearly piss my pants." I decided to ignore the locked door comment. Loren had been part of an elite task force that brought all kinds of supernatural monsters to justice until only a few days ago. "What kind of business?"

Loren was taller than me, with a military haircut and a jaw that could cut you as deep as his words. He didn't take shit but would give you the shirt off his back. Total Slytherin, in my opinion. "I want to know why you've broken your vow to never hunt."

My heart pounded in my ears. *How did he know what I was doing*? He sat up and faced me, folding his hands between his knees.

"It's always suspicious when someone starts ordering a dozen Pandora's boxes at a time. Especially when that someone is having them delivered to Hayvenwood. Under his real name." His eyes narrowed. "So Rune, care to explain?"

The sound of my birthname made my chest tighten. It was used so infrequently, it left me off balance. These were the names our late mother used to call us when we were in the safety of our home. They were safeguarded to prevent their use in summoning spells, hexes, and traps that even a hunter couldn't defeat. They were kept hidden and safe.

"I'm not hunting again," I admitted carefully. "Just...helping."

Loren stood, the bedside lamp casting dark shadows over his near-black eyes. "Every single hunter has to be registered. You know that. Imagine what it felt like to get the call that my own little brother was thought to be disobeying the cardinal rule. Do you know what it took to convince them I could handle it, even though I had already turned in my resignation?"

I swallowed the lump from my throat and shook my head. "I'm sorry."

Loren put his hands on my shoulder. "Tell me what you're doing. We'll figure it out."

Sighing, I shook my head. "I can't—"

"Yes, you can," Loren said, squeezing my shoulders.

"Why are guys so dramatic?" Romi asked as she appeared next to us.

Loren's head snapped over to where she—stood? floated? hovered?—and his hands released me. "Says the ghost who makes dramatic entrances and exits?"

She pursed her lips and pointed at him. "Fair." She gestured between us. "But for real, what's going on here?"

My brother crossed his arms and took a step back to look at Romi. She mirrored his position.

"You know I will win any staring contest, right?" She tilted her head to the side then gestured to her eyes. "I don't blink."

Loren pressed his lips together, clearly trying not to smile. "What are you doing with the Pandora's boxes?"

She shrugged. "I'm not doing anything with them."

Technically not a lie. I was the one doing something with them.

She looked at her nails as if examining her manicure. "If demons just happen to fall into them, it's not my fault. If they happen to be buried in consecrated ground?" She shrugged again. "Pity."

Loren blinked. "Tell me you're joking. How?" He shook his head as if to clear his thoughts. "That's a heavily guarded secret. We aren't even in testing stages—"

She pointed to herself. "Ghost, remember?" Her head

whipped toward the door. "Don't leave the room until I tell you it's okay. Hysin's partner is pissed." Without warning, she disappeared.

"That will never not be creepy," Loren muttered before rushing over to the window and pushing the blackout curtain aside to peer out. He reached for the door handle, but I knocked him away.

"Don't."

He brushed my hand away. "I'm not letting your girl-friend fight a demon for me. Especially since we just fought off Noiran."

I stepped between him and the door. "You can die. She can't. Let her fight."

Loren lifted his hands up in surrender and walked back to the bed, then sat down. He rubbed his buzzed head with his palm. "How am I supposed to report this?"

I sat down next to him. "What do you mean?"

Loren studied me for a long moment. "Romi isn't anything I've ever seen before. She's not a ghost in the traditional sense, and she's not a poltergeist. She's nearly solid some nights and smoke others." His thumb tapped against this knee. "No ghost has ever fought a demon and won. And she has top-secret information."

I frowned, rolling his words over in my mind.

"How many?"

I counted off my mental list. "Four boxes so far, but she's hunted down fourteen demons since Halloween. I don't know how many before that. Sends them away limping to recover."

"Fourteen?!" Loren stared at me incredulously. He ran a hand down his face. "Fuck."

"What?"

"I thought..." He shook his head. He stood and started to pace. "I think I missed the clues right in front of me."

"Like what?"

Romi flashed into the room, wiping her hands off on her jeans. "Why are demons so sticky?" she grumbled. She looked at me and then Loren. "Did I interrupt something?"

Loren shook his head, gave me a brief hug, then pulled his cell from his pocket and started dialing as he walked out the door. "No, I'll talk to you later."

I cleared my throat, trying to ease the tickle of anxiety. "How'd it go?"

She smiled and walked over to me, lacing her cold fingers through mine. "Easy peasy. That demon wasn't worth the energy. Shoved her through a portal."

She stepped closer. "Look at you. You're still dirty from the cemetery." She leaned against my chest and I placed my hand against her nearly completely solid back. Despite the accompanying goosebumps, fire flicked to life underneath my skin at her nearness.

"Well, we better shower," I growled.

She gave me a wicked smile and disappeared. A moment later, the shower turned on. I put the safety lock on the door and then pulled off my shirt, making my way to the bathroom. My eyes roamed over the smiling woman who leaned against the doorframe, watching me unbutton my pants, and I couldn't stop Loren's words from repeating in my head.

Romi isn't anything I've ever seen before.

3

ROMI

I looked around incredulously, confused how one moment I was snuggled next to my boyfriend—mortal half? *Mon gran matou*? (quite frankly, I think "my big male cat" is adorable)—and the next I was in the middle of Hell. This was probably very, very bad. There was no street sign or anything announcing where I was, but there was a distinct smell here that I could never forget as long as I unlived.

It was true what you died in became what you wore in the afterlife. Thank god I was in a t-shirt, hoodie, and jeans. I pulled the shirt up and over my nose. It didn't really help because I couldn't really smell. I just absorbed the scent because Hell was obnoxious like that.

Why was I here? Did I have frequent flyer miles or something? A visitor's badge? Why couldn't I visit a French patisserie or an amusement park instead?

I stood on a gravel path that snaked through the cave. Ash rained down from the blackness above, coating the ground in an eerie, snow-like gray. Pools of perfectly still water lined the edges of the pathway, black as midnight.

There was no music in Hell, no ambient noise. No water rushing, no wind blowing. It was negative sound, so quiet it was painful. Except, of course, for the screams and harried breathing of those begging for mercy.

There was no daylight or artificial lighting, but somehow there was enough ambient glow to see clearly. An endless row of doors set into the cave walls lined the edge of the shadows. Each door was different in color and size. Some were three-car garages, others were tiny cubbyholes. To my left, a decorative bronze door sat next to a bedroom door with children's drawings taped all over it.

Without thinking, I walked toward the drawings, fingering the paper. The door opened a few inches, leaving me enough room to look inside. A man knelt on the ground facing the door, a gas can in one hand, a lighter in the other. Behind him were bunk beds, piled high with blankets.

The pungent odor of gasoline seeped from every crevasse of the room as the man sloshed it from a rusted gas can. He stood in the center of the room and looked toward the ceiling, not noticing the liquid dumping onto his legs and shoes. "Please," he said, his voice cracking. Huge beads of sweat poured down his lobster red face while his whole body trembled. "Make it stop."

He cried out as his body moved seemingly without his permission, dropping the gas can and pulling a matchbook from his pocket. His hopeless eyes met mine, his entire body shaking with the movement. "Run," he mouthed.

I slammed the door shut as he lit the match. His gut-wrenching screams echoed in my brain moments before a ball of flames engulfed the door. Then it was gone, and the cell reset. Suddenly, the same man was outside, walking in with a can of gasoline. He didn't even seem to notice me as he twisted the knob and stepped inside.

I closed my eyes and walked past, unable to stomach seeing the flames again. Hell didn't have to try hard to torture people; all it had to do was make you relive the worst, most shameful moment of your life over and over again. If you were lucky and escaped your guilt—somehow found a way to forgive yourself—you had the chance to wander this hallway and watch other people relive their moments.

It was brilliant in its simplicity.

If you could escape your cell, if you could walk out of the cave entrance and get to a portal, you were golden. Little known fact—you can leave Hell and escape to the non-tortured afterlife, as long as you didn't become a snack for a demon or a cannibalistic plant. I had escaped once before, but I wasn't sure I could do it again. Not if I was more than just a visitor here.

My feet stopped moving, an unknown force wrapping around me and pulling me backward. I didn't need to open my eyes to know where I was, but I did anyway. A dog door swung back and forth on the bright red door, and my old black lab, Gus, poked his head out and barked a greeting. His tongue hung out the side of his mouth.

My fingers flexed at my side, desperate to pet his head. "Hey, boy," I called, following with a low whistle. He barked again and his whole body wiggled, like it always did when he wagged his tail.

As I reached out to touch him, a small but sharp warning from a memory long ago pushed its way forward. *Don't.* I let my hand drop and took a step back. Gus's head cocked to the side, his eyes pleading.

"I'm sorry, boy," I whispered and took two steps backward.

He let out a bark that sounded like a chainsaw layered

with a thousand screams, before leaping from the door and morphing into a creature that looked more than like a red-eyed wolf made out of ash than a household pet. Fear wrapped itself so tight around me, I almost couldn't remember how to move.

Run, that little voice in my head warned.

I ran down the gravel paths and around sharp corners. The labyrinth here was endless and chaotic. Pathways would suddenly change or disappear, Hell ultimately deciding where it wanted me to go. I was simply a pawn in a celestial chess game, and I couldn't tell if I was winning or losing.

My steps faltered as I passed the same turquoise-blue front door for the fourth time. It looked like it was bathed in the summer sun. There was a gorgeous wreath of sunflowers holding a "welcome home" sign. The sight of such a beautiful, peaceful thing inside of literal Hell made me want to cry. Whatever was behind that door was going to be heartbreaking.

As I turned to walk away, that voice inside stopped me. *Open*. Honestly, I wasn't sure if that was my subconscious reliving my time here or if it was a trick of this place, but I listened to it. Probably a stupid idea.

The door latch felt substantial in my hand and I gasped, jumping backward and cradling my hand against my chest. Why could I feel that? How could I feel that? I hadn't felt anything but *cold* in three years. Why here? Why now?

Romi, you can do this, I told myself. *Big ghost pants on. Open the door in three...two...one...*

With bravery I didn't know I possessed, I disengaged the latch and pushed the door open. Careful not to physically step over the threshold, I leaned in and froze. A scream I couldn't contain ripped out of me.

Inside of the beautiful door was a woman surrounded by demons, a woman I recognized by the pictures each of the Lynch brothers put around their rooms. Laura Lynch stared at me with unseeing eyes. She was still as death, except for the tortured pleading pouring out of her mouth. She was standing in a beautiful field, but whatever they were making her relive over and over again was insidious.

I closed the door quickly, dry heaving. There was no relief in the action, but I couldn't not do it. I cried without tears, angry that I had no way to release the knot in my unmoving chest. I knew these cells intimately. I had survived escaping once.

Hell locked you in a room and played your most shameful memory—the one you felt the guiltiest about—on repeat. You relived each second until you were out of your mind. Laura must be trapped in the vicious cycle.

I pressed my hand to my stomach trying to find the strength to go in and save her. Why was she here? Was it because she helped kill a demon to save her sons and Hayvenwood? Where was Raine's mom, Genevieve? She had helped, too, according to Raine.

A beautiful frosted glass door lit up in front of me and I could hear piano music hovering in the air around it. The song was familiar, a favorite of Raine's. She played it every time she worked at Billy's. With a sinking feeling of dread, I opened the door to spot a woman who looked exactly like her daughter, only twenty-odd years older, sitting on a piano bench. An apparition who looked exactly like Raine sat next to her, playing.

Genevieve was frozen in wide-eyed terror as something I couldn't see played out in front of her. She cried silently, tears coming from all four corners of her eyes. Something flew over my head and into the doorway, stopping in front of me. I recognized her energy immediately as Hysin's partner, Solka.

She screamed and lunged. I swore she said, "You killed him!" but I couldn't make out the words. They were too loud and too sharp. I took off running, Solka racing behind me.

A perfectly still pond appeared in front of me and without a second thought, I jumped into a cannonball. I splashed and fell through the veil, rolling onto the grimy carpet in Fenton's hotel room.

He sat up immediately and turned on the bedside lamp and leaped from the bed. He looked around in a panic before his eyes settled on me. "Romi!" He ran over and crouched in front of me, his blue eyes—Laura's eyes—roaming over my face and body, checking for damage. "Babe, what's wrong?"

I tried to talk, but the words got stuck.

"Rosemary, talk to me. Please."

"I had a nightmare."

He paled. "But you don't sleep."

"I know."

His fingers traced my cheekbone and it was a fleeting moment of pressure. "What about?"

I grabbed his wrist and pressed his entire palm against the side of my cheek, needing to feel something other than completely and utterly dead. "Your mom and Raine's mom. They're trapped in Hell."

I flickered out of the room and into the in-between for a few seconds and then back into the hotel room, as if someone had turned off a light switch and turned it back on. I stared at Fenton. "That's probably not good."

"What's going on?"

"I don't know," I whispered. "Probably just a bad dream."

4

FENTON

Two days later, I met my brothers at Billy's Blues and BBQ, or at least what was left of it. We had worked with the local police to make sure most of the residents were either back in their homes or at the motel until repairs could be done. I was exhausted but hopeful.

Romi had been having nightmares continuously since the storm ended, and honestly, it freaked me out. I had kept myself on the edge of sleep as long as possible to make sure she was okay, which was pretty much impossible as she was a ghost. I tipped back my to-go cup of coffee from Roasted and finished the last, bitter drops. I hated coffee, but I was going to need it to get through today. Stepping around a pile of shingles that had been ripped off the roof in the demonic-winter-storm, I ducked under the caution tape roping off the cracked front door and made my way inside the bar.

Remnants of this place being a make-shift shelter still littered the ground. Blankets were piled high, and empty water bottles and food wrappers lined the floor. Tarps covered holes in the ceiling, although it did nothing to keep the cold at bay. It looked desperate and broken, kind of like me.

"It's hard to believe anything bad happened here."

I turned to see Loren walking in. "Yeah," I replied. "It feels like a bad dream."

He came over and gave me a quick hug and thump on the back. "Is Grayson here?" Grayson was the middle brother in our trio, who was madly in love with Romi's *alive* twin sister, Hazel.

As if on cue, Grayson, Hazel, and an older man, who I assumed was Billy, walked in through the kitchen. I could tell by their expressions that the news was bad. Loren shifted so his chin was a little higher and his shoulders a little straighter, transforming from concerned brother to the man who leads missions all over the globe.

Hazel hugged the man with the graying hair for a long moment, before stepping back and turning her head to wipe her eyes. My heart sank. This place made Hazel truly happy and I knew what it was like to have your home pulled out from under your feet.

Grayson made his way over while Hazel walked the man to the door. "That was Billy."

Loren raised his eyebrow, waiting for him to continue. Instead, Grayson turned his body toward Hazel and reached out his hand. She came over, taking it and squeezing so tight, her knuckles went white.

"He'll call me later, but I think he's selling," Hazel explained, her voice cracking on the last word, betraying her emotion.

Grayson released her hand and pulled her into the side of his body. "Billy's insurance company is being an asshole."

Hazel wiped under her eye with the edge of her shirt-sleeve. "I need to go home and think," she explained quietly.

Grayson nodded and kissed the side of her forehead and whispered something into her ear. "Let me get her home, we'll need to get a plywood patch on this roof, and we'll see what we can do around town. Has anyone checked on the church?"

Loren nodded. "Yeah. Javier went out this morning with Jimmy. All church activities have been moved to the high school gym for the moment."

Grayson looked between us and rubbed his thumb against his first two fingers—the sign for money. Both Loren and I tipped our chins up. We were going to make a few large donations from our inheritances. With the right financial leverage, a new church could be erected by spring and the town's repairs could start right away. After all, it was kind of our fault it exploded in the first place.

As soon as they left, Loren looked me over. "So...we going to talk about it?"

I flinched. "Nothing really to talk about. I'm just there to hold the box." I wanted to tell him about the so-called nightmares that Romi had been having for the last few days, but without her here, I didn't know how to explain it. Honestly, she didn't even really explain it to me.

We didn't talk as I grabbed trash bags from storage, then sorted through everything left behind. A teddy bear, a retainer, a few sweatshirts, and several gloves, went into the "keep" pile with the stack of blankets. We'd need to track down the owners soon.

It was freezing; while the apocalyptic snowstorm was gone—causing massive confusion all over the weather stations—Michigan's upper peninsula in November was still a force to be reckoned with.

"I'm so tired of being cold," I grumbled, my teeth practically chattering.

Loren gave me a long look. "Well, for starters, gloves would help." He pulled a second pair—identical to the ones he was wearing—out of his pocket and tossed them to me.

They were thick and fleece lined, and the feeling in my fingers slowly returned. "Thanks."

"Also, you need a real hat. We grew up in Maine. How have you forgotten how to winter?"

I shrugged. "I hate the cold. Hence me moving to a state without winter."

The crease between his eyes deepened. "Been meaning to ask you about that. What are your long-term plans?"

"Do I need them?"

Loren opened his mouth but stayed silent when the front door opened. Grayson and Javier walked in carrying disposable coffee cups. Javier handed a cup to Loren and Grayson extended one to me. "It's chai with that fake milk shit."

I smiled and gave him a silent toast. One sip and my insides started to thaw. "Thanks."

Javier surveyed the now clean Billy's and then hopped up on the counter. "They have a team of fifteen at the church right now, sifting through rubble to try and save whatever they can. Eggs 'N Oinks is relatively undamaged—just a few cracked windows. Hayvenwood Mobile Home Park has some damage, but the neighbors are all helping out." He pulled out an actual paper map from his back pocket. "This street, however, has significant damage and the homeowner's insurance is unlikely to be helpful."

"Why?" I asked. As someone who lived in short-term leases or motels, homeowner's insurance wasn't something I completely understood.

Javier gave me a sad smile. "Because most of them didn't have any or enough. The residents are mostly elderly, living on social security and what little pensions remain."

Grayson pointed up. "Billy brought in some plywood. Help me get it on the roof to prevent more damage, then we'll hit that street."

After a freezing—and quite frankly, terrifying—roof job, we made our way to Millicent Creek Drive, our trucks filled with toolboxes, shovels, blankets, gravel, salt, contractor-grade trash bags, a ladder, and whatever else they could think to add. I made fun of Grayson when I saw how much random junk he had, but Loren just beamed with pride. This was another gene that wasn't passed down to me.

Everything I owned was transitory. The only reason I even owned a shovel was because I had bought one last week. Life was fleeting and I hated being tied down to one place. It made me itchy. Attached. Roots were for people who weren't comfortable with being on their own.

Sure, I loved being with my brothers. They were the people I loved most in this world. I wanted us all to be together, but I wanted us all to be together while not giving up the rest of our lives to a dingy, small town.

We turned on Millicent and into the first driveway. Tree branches and limbs littered the yard; one had come down on the gutter, pulling it halfway off the house. Another had taken out the porch step. Ice coated everything, including the dented garage door. A strange prickling crawled over my skin, just like the moment before Romi appeared. I looked around but didn't see her.

Loren jumped out of the truck and knocked on the door. It creaked open as a woman, who was barely up to Loren's chest, peeked out. She smiled and extended her hand. "Lucian, it's wonderful to see you again." She stood up on her tiptoes and kissed both his cheeks. And he let her.

My eyes widened at not only the use of Loren's birth-name but also the fact that this woman *kissed his cheeks*.

Javier walked over and put his fingers under my jaw, closing it. "Forgot to mention this street is full of Others."

I raised an eyebrow. "I've never seen him that nice to anyone," I muttered.

"Then you don't really know your brother," he replied before opening the back of Loren's Yukon and starting to pull out the tools.

His words dug into my skin and I bit my cheeks, wanting to yell back, "well they don't know me, either!" but restraining myself. Two years apart, and they felt like strangers. The last time we were together, we were staring at Dad's lifeless body.

The image was still the last thing I saw before I fell asleep. The guilt that lived with me never went away. I could have stopped him. Gone with him. Died with him.

Demon. It was strange to me, how my father who hunted witches was killed by a demon. But then, Loren wasn't really a witch hunter, either. The familiar anger that followed my confusion burned my chest as we got to work salting the driveway and cleaning up the yard. Everything I thought I knew about my family had been turned on its head since our reunion.

I watched Grayson wielding a chainsaw and cutting up a large tree limb that could be used for firewood. He had protected me since we were kids, going on hunts for me so I didn't have to harm another person. Why, then, had he never told me about the other kind of hunting?

I didn't want to kill innocent people who were only witches because they were born that way. Hating someone because of something they couldn't control was preposterous. Putting away terrible monsters and getting rid of demons triggered something inside of me. My instinct to protect, my birthright as a hunter.

Would knowing that I could be loved and respected by Others, instead of only feared and hated, change any part of my life? What if I hadn't cut off all communication with them? What if I had listened when Loren had tried to call me, and presumably Grayson, too?

I thumped my chest with my fist and got back to work. *You never expected to see them again*, I told myself. *It's okay to feel conflicted.* I swallowed hard and let my mind think the even scarier truth. *What if they find out that you killed Dad?*

A hand touched my shoulder and I jumped, dropping the bundle of branches. My cheeks tingled as they warmed, and for once, my blush was welcome because I couldn't feel my face. I turned to find a smirking Loren standing next to a large man with russet hair and bushy beard. He blinked at me and I startled to see his eyes transition from regular human pupils to reptilian, then back again.

"Fenton, this is Henry Jackson. Helped us out during the storm."

I accepted his offered hand and we shook. I was no slouch, but I was pretty sure his grip almost broke my hand. After he released me, I flexed my fingers twice to make sure they weren't broken.

He chuckled. "Sorry about that. I sometimes forget how strong I am."

If this line came from anyone other than a supernatural creature, I would have had to knee them in the nuts on principle. Instead, I just smiled and nodded. "No harm done. Nice to meet you. And thanks for saving my brothers."

"My pleasure." He gestured across the street. "My guys and I are finishing up across the street and I wanted to stop and see if you needed anything. Figured we can get a few more houses in before dark."

Loren gestured to the house we were working on. "We're almost done here. Need to come back with some parts for the garage and the gutter, but the temporary fixes should hold for now."

Henry looked over the work and nodded. "Looks good. The hardware store is closed for the day—Gerard is out helping at the church—but if you leave him a voicemail, he'll get you what you need." He turned to me. "Tell that friend of yours I appreciate what she's doing, but she needs to be careful. Staying hidden is what keeps us safe." He blinked again and I was shocked a second time at how his eye changed from human to reptilian, then back again.

"Friend?" I asked stupidly. The eye had really distracted me.

"The one who fought the demon?" He tugged on his beard. "I'm all for getting rid of the bastards, but fighting one in daylight on the street was risky." He stared at me for a long moment. "A ghost, well, that's not something we usually see around here. Never know what people will do when they face something unfamiliar..."

The warning turned my insides as cold as the cutting wind. It didn't take a genius to figure out what people tended to do when they experienced unfamiliar things, only someone who ever read a history book.

Loren's eyes held mine. "Thanks, Henry. We'll take care of it," he promised. They shook hands and then Loren walked him to the edge of the driveway, talking quietly.

My head spun with Henry's words. *How could they hurt Romi? Could they even touch her? What were the rules of a ghost witch?*

I pulled off my glove and grabbed a tissue out of my

pocket to wipe my frozen nose. It was so cold, even my nose hairs had icicles. When I shoved the tissue back into my pocket, I noticed my cell vibrating. Grabbing it, I read the text message.

Hazel: Everyone free to meet at Billy's, 6pm?

Looking around, I saw my brothers and Javier looking at their phones. I replied with a thumbs-up emoji, put my phone away, and shoved my glove back on. Loren walked back over and helped me pile the branches and trash bags at the end of the driveway for pick up later.

"How can they hurt Romi?" I asked without preamble.

He finished piling the bags together and surveyed the work before speaking. "I don't know," he finally admitted. "If she were a normal ghost, I'd guess something like a séance or exorcism. If she were an actual witch, Pandora's box or a spell to bind her..."

"But as a witch ghost?"

"Honestly, I'm not even sure that's what she is." Javier called his name and he lifted his hand in a "one moment" gesture. "I don't know how to protect her." He gripped my shoulder. "But we'll figure it out."

5

Ghosts were never punctual. Time was a human construct, measuring the space between moments. When you were dead, all you had was space. After attending my favorite, although somewhat frustrating, French class—seriously people, it's not that hard to say, "My first class is in the math building on the east end of campus" (*Mon premier cours a lieu dans le bâtiment de maths, côté est du campus*)—I found Hazel getting ready for a staff meeting at Billy's.

My sister looked just like me—long, dark hair (although hers had a white streak), our mother's nose, our father's jaw, fair skin—but her eyes were purple, identifying her as a practicing witch. The day I died, my eyes changed back to blue. As she pulled her hair back into a braid and put on mascara, I longed to feel her fingers on my scalp or fight over the bathroom mirror just one more time.

I followed her to the bar, then watched with quiet longing as everyone shared food and drinks. What I wouldn't give for a cheeseburger, extra pickles. Hazel, staring at her untouched glass of whiskey, finally admitted, "Billy wants to sell."

If I had a beating heart, it would've broken. This place was her home. It was what made her happy and made her money. Not for the first time, I simmered in my own anger.

Maybe this was purgatory. Sure, I escaped Hell, but now I was forced to watch the people I love struggle and be physically unable to help them. Raine suggesting that they all pitch in and buy Billy's should've made me ecstatic, but I just got more frustrated.

This was *my* sister. I should be the one helping her. I rubbed my head as if I had a headache, which was impossible since I was a ghost. A goddamn ghost.

Fenton leaned close to my ear, although he didn't need to. I could hear him whether or not he was across the room or practically on top of me. "What's wrong?"

I crossed my arms and tried to appear calm. "Nothing. Everything's fine."

"You're a terrible liar."

I shrugged and pretend to listen to Raine and Hazel talk about how they could make Billy's an even more attractive live music hangout. Dean, the day shift manager, and his boyfriend Alex, who worked in the kitchen and bussed tables, were concerned about making Hayvenwood a more public place. Dean wore a bright pink cast from his fingers to his shoulder and healing dark brown scrapes covered his skin. Alex's leg started bouncing under the table and he chewed on his bottom lip. While most of us had only psychological scars from the demon attack, they still had a very bright physical reminder.

"What happens when they kidnap us and sell us as oddities?" Dean asked.

Loren sat up straighter in his chair. "I would never let that happen."

Something moved in my peripheral vision and I swung my head toward the bar. I swear I saw a dog's tail. I disappeared into the in-between, trying to catch a shadow, but saw nothing.

When I returned to my seat, Fenton stared at me. "Now you're being really weird," he whispered.

"I thought I saw something, but I was wrong," I explained. I knew I wasn't wrong but now was not the time.

"The dogs again?"

"Absolutely not." Now I was outright lying. I had been seeing what I thought were dogs since I'd returned from Hell. It didn't make sense and was really starting to freak me out.

"That means yes," he said quietly. "You need to tell them," he said a little louder.

Raine leaned forward and tapped on the table to get our attention. "Romi, what?" Her white-blonde hair with the blue tips was piled high on her head, her pale skin still red with windburn from the storm.

Dammit. I glared at Fenton before shaking my head. "Nothing." What was I going to tell them, that I kept seeing weird creatures just out of sight? Freak everyone out?

Fenton's phone buzzed on the table and he silenced it, but not before I saw the motel's name and number come up. That was odd. Why would they be calling?

"No, it's something," Fenton argued then looked to Galinda. "Maybe you can help." He narrowed his eyes at me and mouthed, *the dogs.*

Galinda tilted her head to the side as if to hear better. Her tight red curls shifted with the movement, her purple eyes accessing.

Fenton bumped his shoulder against mine encouragingly and I scrunched my face in frustration. "Fine!" I took a deep breath, out of habit over necessity, and let my arms fall to my lap. "I've..." Another shadow—another dog?—ran right behind Hazel. "...been having dreams, since Raine came back."

"Dreams?" Raine asked, confused.

At her question, I focused back on the conversation and winced. That wasn't what I was going to say. Well, I was in it now. "About your mom and Laura. They're trapped in Hell." I nearly facepalmed myself. *Way to be sensitive, Romi.*

Fenton stiffened, then reached over to squeeze my hand reassuringly. Well, as much as one can squeeze a ghost hand.

Loren stared at me. "It's probably just leftover stress from the storm," he said, his voice too even. I would've believed his calm demeanor if he hadn't paled under his deeply tanned skin. I could feel his unspoken words. *I don't want Raine to worry about her mom.*

"They did kill a demon," Raine whispered. "What if...?" Her pale fingers moved across the table as if playing a silent piano.

Grayson threw his hand in the air, although his gray eyes were glued on Loren. By the way his ears turned red, I had a suspicion he could read Loren's silent conversation, too. "They're just nightmares from Raine sharing her story, Romi." He rubbed the back of his neck, tugging at his dark, shaggy hair. His nervous tell. He knew something was wrong.

"You guys don't get it. Forget it." I was hoping my nonchalant brush off would work, but it came off way more angsty and less easy-breezy. I sucked at lying.

Grayson, Loren, and Fenton exchanged a silent conversation. It lasted only a few seconds, but it was vicious.

"Just tell them," Fenton sighed. His phone vibrated again, and he ignored it, tucking it away in his hoodie pocket.

I wanted to tell him to answer the call. It felt *important*. I touched his wrist, but he shook my head and mouthed *later*.

"Rosemary Evanora, speak," Hazel ordered. Her words were sharp and clipped, but her emotions were loud and billowing. She was scared, upset, and worried. Her emotions clung to the air like bad perfume swirling around me tighter and tighter.

Another shadow darted alongside Loren. Two more outside the bar's cracked glass door. For the first time since I had escaped Hell, I was afraid.

"I don't sleep, Zee!" I practically yelled, totally freaked out. "I'm dead, remember? How am I even dreaming?" As soon as the words were out, it was like the room stopped to take a breath. Even the shadows disappeared. I let my hands fall and reveled in the momentary silence. It was all out there now, no more hiding.

Galinda moved first, coming over and leaning so close that I could count the dark brown freckles on her light brown skin. Tentatively, she reached up and caressed my shoulder. She let her hand drop as if she couldn't concentrate on moving it where she wanted. "I haven't...I don't..."

She took a deep sniff and let her fingers trail along my shoulder, before bringing them to her lips. Her eyes widened and she shook her head, as if in disbelief. "Forgive my bluntness, but you're not a ghost."

If I could feel panic, I would one hundred percent be freaking out right now. This had been my greatest fear, my biggest suspicion. I hadn't been able to transition from life

HEATHER NOVAK

to afterlife, even after escaping Hell. I never saw any other spirits, not fully formed humans like me anyway. I just wandered aimlessly around, staying tethered to first Hazel and now Fenton, trying to figure out why it was taking more and more energy to appear for shorter bursts of time.

If I wasn't a ghost, then what was I? I tried to keep a calm demeanor by pursing my lips and lifting my eyebrow. "I died in a car accident when I was eighteen," I defended. "I was there."

Galinda shook her head. "No, I mean, you aren't dead, Rosemary. You're cursed." She paused. "Not completely dead, anyway. You are trapped between the living and the dead."

Cursed. Trapped.

The words wrapped themselves around me and settled deep inside. "But I died," I whispered. "I fulfilled the terms!" I grabbed her arm, pleading with her. "I fulfilled the terms..."

She didn't respond, only took in my stricken face with a terrible sadness. The only sound was Hazel's chair screeching across the linoleum floor. I turned to see her standing there, muscles locked and eyes fierce. I could see the shadows of cracks forming underneath her skin, as if everything that held her together was only moments away from shattering.

"Rosemary." Her voice shook.

If I was alive, I'd cry. My throat would grow tight and my chest clogged with emotions. Instead, I just felt *wrong*. Like someone had separated me from a battery and reattached me the wrong way. I grew more translucent, struggling to find enough energy.

Fenton's arm wrapped around me. "Use me."

I pulled more of his energy to stay. He was warm and

comforting, and I had to restrain myself from using too much, too fast.

Grayson stood and put his hand on Hazel's waist, pulling her into his side. "Galinda, what does this mean? How is she cursed? It can be broken, right?"

Galinda nodded. "Death, in theory, completes the cycle." Her purple eyes studied me, trying to find an answer. "But it didn't, for you. Why?"

Loren tapped his knuckles on the table, thinking. "Not all curses are broken by death. If it's hereditary, it's passed through blood, although there have been cases of it passing to spouses or adopted children. If it's retribution, depending on the spell used and the strength of the caster, it can hang on after death, but it starts to fade immediately without a living soul to feed it." He frowned, trying to reach for an answer that he didn't have.

"Unless it's devil magic," Javier offered quietly.

Galinda and Javier looked between each other, then back at me. I didn't have to say anything out loud. Whatever Galinda saw on my face confirmed her suspicion. "The cycle wouldn't be complete until they both died."

The bottom fell out of my ethereal world. *Both*. I shook my head. "No, I read that journal over and over again." I was starting to grow fuzzy around the edges. "There was nothing...I already paid them!" They were going to take everything from me.

I gave up my life to save my father's, and now the only way to be free was to wait for the man I sacrificed everything for to die? Energy pulsed through me and I flashed between the color of this world and the black and white of the in-between over and over again. I was spiraling, unable to focus on staying anywhere.

The dogs were back, running in and out of color, their

eyes flashing red before they disappeared. I covered my eyes and screamed. Everything tethering me to this spot released and I fell into darkness.

When I opened my eyes, I was staring at that same blue door again, back in Hell.

6

There were no words to describe what we had all just witnessed, or at least none that I could find. It was like watching a projected film image melt and curl in on itself. I stood so fast, my chair fell backward. "Romi?!"

Hazel ran around the table to where Romi last stood, her eyes huge and terrified. "Where is she?!" she shouted.

"This is how her nightmares start," I admitted quietly. "But worse." *Much worse.* I refused to even think about her being in Hell with my wonderful mother. It would break me. "Why are they getting worse?"

Galinda put her hand on my arm. "We'll figure it out."

Alex and Dean stood and put on their coats. Dean walked over to Hazel and touched her arm. "This is a family affair, so we'll leave you in privacy. Please let us know how we can support you." She didn't respond, just kept staring at the floor. "Tiff, come on, honey. We'll give you a ride."

Tiffany, who had come with Hazel and Grayson, grabbed her coat and all but sprinted after them. Javier followed

35

them to the door to lock it behind them. Hazel still didn't move.

"I've got you," Grayson whispered against her temple.

Two tears ran down her cheeks. "I don't understand," she finally whispered.

I closed my eyes and took a deep breath, wanting more than anything to be the person who didn't have to tell this story. "I do." Everyone turned to stare at me, and the food I had eaten turned to cement in my stomach.

After our first introduction, Romi surprised me in my motel room. I was halfway to drunk, trying unsuccessfully to forget that I had been kidnapped, I had killed my father, and my brothers were back and going to find out the truth.

She appeared cross-legged on the messy double bed in front of me. "You let me know when you find it," she said.

"What?"

"Whatever you think is at the bottom of that bottle." She touched the label, then whistled and shook her head. "Don't ever let my sister see you drink that."

I shrugged. "Cheap or expensive get me drunk exactly the same."

She groaned and rolled her eyes. "Why are men so dramatic?" She moved closer to me. No, moved wasn't the right word. Floated? Appeared? "I think you and I have a lot in common."

Sweat pricked the back of my neck and I shivered hard, once. The ghost's blue eyes were gentle but prodding, like a needle poking into flesh looking for the poisonous stinger. Those eyes somehow pulled the truth from my lips. "I killed my father."

"See? We're practically soulmates already. I killed my father, too."

I blinked, hard. "Uh...wasn't your father the one who just kidnapped me?"

She shrugged. "I didn't say he stayed dead."

I blinked away the memory and took a deep breath, then looked into Hazel's eyes. "Your dad had accidentally ingested peanuts and the epinephrine failed. Romi only had moments to make the decision..." As I told her the story, at least as much as I knew, color drained from her face.

She swayed on her feet and Grayson caught her, lowering her to a chair. Raine jumped up, poured her a glass of water, and crouched down beside her, trying to coax her to drink.

Loren stood and walked over to Galinda, me, and Javier. "What are the options? How do we break it besides killing their father?"

Galinda was going through her phone, searching through pages of text. "I don't know. I don't know what spell book she used or who helped her." She made a frustrated noise and tapped the screen violently. "It's more complicated than just killing Blaze, now that he's stripped of his powers. If he dies right now, the cycle ends. The curse isn't 'broken', it's 'completed'. She'll remain dead, but she'll cross over into the afterlife at least."

She pulled her glasses out of her pocket and put them on her nose, mouthing the words as she read. "If we can get his powers reinstated, then do a sacrificial spell, it should break the curse and give Romi her life back."

Javier mumbled a stream of Spanish, including several words that I knew were profanity.

"What?" I asked.

Loren pinched the bridge of his nose. "We'd have to do some very illegal shit to get them back."

"And who'd do the sacrificial spell?" Javier asked. "Without a gray witch, who would do that much dark magic?"

Galinda put her phone in her pocket and removed her

glasses. "We'd have to get both Blaze and Ginger their powers back. Ginger is so addicted to dark magic, you know she'd do anything to touch it again. Just don't tell her what the spell is for. Strip her of her powers immediately following. The girls live happily ever after as humans."

He ran a hand over his face. "Fuck, Galinda."

She crossed her arms. "You asked me what the options were without a gray witch, not for a bedtime story."

I wanted to scream and cry and burn everything to the fucking ground. We had a gray witch, right here, until four days ago. But Raine had given up her powers to save my brothers and this town, and now no one knew the location of another gray witch. "So there's no hope, unless..." I used a hand gesture to finish the sentence. *Murder their father, torture their mother.*

Hazel shook her head. "Whatever you need to do to save my sister," she whispered. I stared at her in absolute shock. Hazel looked more broken, more hopeless than I had ever seen her. This is what Grayson meant when he said he couldn't take her powers because if Hazel lost her twin, it would destroy her.

Galinda looked away but not before I saw the shininess of her eyes. "I mean, the only other way that might work—and it's only a theory—is a kiss from her true love."

I blinked then frowned. "Assuming that I am her true love, I can't actually kiss her. She's a ghost."

She nodded. "Exactly. You could try a soul-releasing spell. As long as you were properly tethered, your soul could theoretically be released—"

"Over my fucking dead body," Loren growled.

I glared at him. "This isn't a choice you get to make." I looked at Galinda. "I'll do it."

Javier pointed at Galinda. "But she can't. It's against HQ policy. Even if it wasn't, we wouldn't cross Loren like that."

Galinda touched my arm. "I can't risk doing it." She nodded toward Hazel. "It's a tough spell. Hazel could do it with a lot of practice…"

My rage burned so hot that my eyes stung. Without even bothering with my coat, I turned away and walked out the front door. I welcomed the icy wind as it sliced through the deep darkness of fall.

It was a mile to the motel, and I was exhausted, but I wasn't going back in to get a ride. I just hoped I didn't slip on ice or something stupid. I really needed to look into getting a vehicle soon.

As I made my way past a street light, a shadow darted through it. My heart galloped as I stopped and looked directly at the pool of yellow on the asphalt. Nothing was there. Shaking my head at my jumpiness, I continued on, until something brushed my legs.

I started running. Fumbling for my phone, I turned on my flashlight app and looked around. Nothing but pavement lined with brown grass and creepy trees. Then again, a shadow just outside of the light. Then another.

Then headlights.

The car pulled up beside me and I sagged in relief to see it was a police car. The officer rolled down the window and I saw Jimmy, Hazel's friend and the man who helped me file kidnapping charges. "Fenton, I've been trying to get ahold of you. Can I give you a ride?"

I nodded and quickly scrambled into the passenger seat, panting. Glancing out through the window, I didn't see the shadows anymore, only an empty road. "Thanks," I managed, buckling my seatbelt.

He looked over at me. "You okay?"

"This place is just a little creepy at night. Was hanging out with my brothers and decided to run back."

He started driving. "Listen, the motel's been trying to call you, but couldn't get ahold of you. There's been a break-in."

Every muscle tightened. "What?"

"We hardly ever have anything like this happen. Usually just punk teenagers looking for cash." He pulled into the parking lot of Hayvenwood Motel and I saw the door to my room had been cut away from the hinges. "Yours was the only room affected. It was clear they were looking for something and you'll want to document anything that's missing."

I stared mutely at the room. I knew in the pit of my stomach that this wasn't a coincidence or some "punk teenagers," it was a warning. Cautiously, I opened the car door and stood, staring. *Was Romi okay? Was this an attack against her?*

I didn't need to be a genius to know the answer was yes. "Jimmy, can you call my brother Loren while I go in?"

"Do you want me to come with you?"

I shook my head. "I've got it." Closing the car door, I took one step, then another, as if in a haze. I felt violated, angry, invaded. I didn't have much that was worth stealing, but it had been my safe space and that safety bubble was shattered.

Ducking under the caution tape, I stepped into the trashed room. The mattresses had been cut open, the cabinet drawers ripped out, the hanging bar in the closet collapsed, and the television gone. I ran to the closet to find the shovel and the last Pandora's box missing. *Fuck.*

The familiar tickle of another presence warned me that someone Other was in the room.

"Fenton?"

Relief flooded through me as Romi appeared on the

other side of the room. Her eyes were wide and her arms wrapped around her middle. She took a hesitant step toward me, then another, then ran and wrapped herself around me.

She felt nearly solid and I relaxed into her coldness. "I'm here," I whispered. "I'm not going to let anyone hurt you." I knew it wasn't a promise I could make, but I needed to believe that I could keep her from harm.

"They were looking for me."

I put my cheek against the top of her head. "How do you know?"

"I had another nightmare."

I stiffened. "I know."

"I think now that the demons know where I am, it's like a channel has opened up."

I wished I could pull her tighter against me. "What happened?" Her fingers ran up and down my spine and I had to clench my teeth to keep from shivering.

"I was pulled back, to your mom's door. When I escaped again, I landed on this carpet, like I always do. Two men were here I didn't recognize, searching through all your things. They said—" She stopped as if trying to regroup. "When they found the box, they said 'we'll get that ghost bitch for what she did.'"

I lifted my head as Jimmy walked into the room and then took a step back. His gaze went from the woman in my arms to my face and he went pale. Loren, Grayson, and a completely shell-shocked Hazel stepped into the room behind him.

Loren let out a string of expletives, some of the words compounded and quite inventive. Grayson seethed with silent fury, and Hazel just stared at her sister, her arms crossed across her middle the same way Romi did when she was scared. Romi turned out of my arms and appeared in front of her. They wrapped around each other, whispering softly.

Jimmy looked at the two of them, dumbstruck. "But...but your sister died..."

Grayson walked over to him and motioned for them to go back outside. "There are some things we need to talk about. Let's go to the front office, get you a cup of coffee."

Loren stood with his shoulder against mine, staring at the closet. "They took the box." It wasn't a question.

"She says two men were here looking for her."

"Probably demons." He stared at the askew closet door for several more moments before he pulled out his phone and opened an app. "Draw the symbol you're adding to the box."

I used my pointer finger to make the rough shape.

He studied it, frowning in concentration. "I wonder if it's possible..."

"What?"

His eyes found mine. "In reverse, this symbol is used to summon demons. We had the theory that if we inverted it and used it on the box, that it would send a demon back to Hell. Maybe we were wrong."

I narrowed my eyes. "How so?"

"Maybe it's killing them."

My eyes went wide. "If she's killing them, they're going to retaliate."

"Against both of you." He started typing out messages on his phone. "Grab your shit. You're going to stay with one of us."

Romi disappeared from Hazel's arms and reappeared in the center of the room. "Stay inside!" Then she was gone.

7

I was so tired of this half-life, of continuously causing pain to the people I loved. I was even more done with fucking demons. "You're not going to touch them!" I warned the student from my French class—well, the class I haunted—as she sauntered toward me.

Her cold, dark eyes never left mine as I intercepted her path to Fenton's door. "*Bonjour,* Meghan," I said, knowing that this wasn't Meghan anymore. The preppy girl with copper skin and long, black hair now dressed like a vampire in a bad gothic movie. Her hair was cut short and her typically bright sweater had been exchanged for a corset. Her eyes flashed red and a familiar tilt of her mouth gave her away.

"Natalia," I sighed. "I thought I had eviscerated you. Should've put you in a box."

She hissed. "Rosemary, Rosemary, Rosemary, you'll pay for that." Different body, same annoying demon.

"I'm not Beetlejuice. You don't have to say my name three times. You here to get your ass kicked again?"

"Winning one fight doesn't mean you won the war."

43

I crossed my arms and held my position. "Try me."

She pursed her lips and stepped closer. "I don't know why these demons are jerking off to the idea of you. You fucked around in some dark magic and got burned. But"—she shrugged—"don't care. Either you come with me or I kill pretty boy in there as punishment and then take you with me. Your move."

"You can't keep me in Hell."

She smirked, getting so close, her nose brushed against my ear. "Aw, don't be like that. We just want to have a little fun with you, like you seem to be having with us. Might go a few rounds with your lover boy, too. Really spice it up."

The cold inside of me turned to red hot rage. They weren't going to touch Fenton, even if I had to go with her right now and never return. It wasn't the worst idea; Hazel would finally be able to grieve me and find peace. Fenton would find a real human to have a relationship with and I wouldn't have to look over my shoulder for the rest of my existence.

I launched myself at her, both of us tumbling back onto the asphalt. I got my hands around her neck before she rolled us over, dislodging my grip. Her body was physically smaller, but she was an old demon and stronger than me.

As she straddled me, I lifted my legs around and crossed them in front of her, then shoved her away from me. Her head hit the cracked concrete parking block and she groaned. I moved behind her, pulling her into a headlock, trying to suffocate the demon out.

Unexpectedly, I felt a weak pulse beneath the pressure of my arms.

Meghan was still alive.

Gasping, I dropped my arms and took a step back, trying to regroup. Demons treated human skin as expendable clothing. They didn't feed or take care of their hosts, and often forgot that humans had very distinct limitations on what they could do without dying. Meghan must have either just been possessed, or she was a fierce fighter.

I ran at her again, but I'd given Natalia too long to recover. She raised her hand and shoved me back with an invisible force. My body flew like a rag doll into the side of a brick wall. Then she pounced and shoved something into my side.

Pain shot through me and I collapsed to the ground, too stunned to move.

Pain.

I hadn't felt pain since the night of the accident. Well, not physically at least. It was such a foreign feeling that I nearly forgot I needed to get up. Struggling to push myself upright, I faced the demon. "H-how?" I groaned. "How can you hurt me?"

The look on her face confirmed she already knew she had the advantage. "Feeling cold? Maybe a bit numb?" She raised her foot and kicked me in the ribs and my vision blurred. She grabbed me by my hair and pulled me sideways. "You're not the only one who can add a symbol on a weapon." She brandished a knife with carvings on the handle.

"Why don't you leave the human out of this?" I wheezed, my vision growing hazy at the edges. "Just you and me, Nat. Drop that meatsuit and come fight me like you mean it."

She cackled. "You're just trying to save her life. I'm onto you, Evanora."

I shrugged. "Noiran couldn't beat me in demon form. I'm pretty sure we both know you won't beat me either. That's why you're using a human shield."

Her eyes burned red and she leaned her head back,

screaming. A dark cloud oozed from her mouth, eyes, ears, and nose until she collapsed onto the asphalt, completely still. *Don't die on me now,* I pleaded with whoever was listening.

Natalia was little more than a shadow in the vague shape of a human. Without wasting a second, she launched herself at me and we tangled. The coldness was spreading, and the pain was staggering, filling me with fear.

The world around us transitioned from color to gray and back to color and I knew I was losing. Natalia wrapped herself around my spirit and started crushing all warmth from me. She held the knife against my throat, and I knew I wasn't going to win this fight without a miracle.

That miracle came in the form of Galinda throwing open her motel door and shooting a small pistol at the demon. Natalia wailed and released me, turning to rush Galinda. Galinda unrolled a burlap cloth with several symbols painted on it. She lit a candle and started chanting, trapping Natalia in an invisible cage as soon her form passed over the cloth. She made an unholy sound as Galinda blew out the candle.

Natalia disappeared back to hell, for the time being. The spell wouldn't keep her from the human world for long, but it was long enough to save Meghan's life.

I hobbled over to Meghan, who was starting to stir. If I had a heart, it would've skipped a beat. "She's still alive."

Jimmy must have seen the fight, because he was already running toward us, waving to the ambulance pulling into the parking lot. I tried to lift Meghan's head from the ground and cradle it in my lap. "Stay with me, help is coming."

Fenton shouted my name, his voice breaking with emotion. My body was throbbing with pain and I looked down, seeing red scratches down my arm and dark stains seeping through my t-shirt.

"I'm bleeding," I said quietly, pressing my hands to my stomach and pulling them away to see red. My eyes went wide and met his, before everything went gray. I fell into the in-between, not wanting him to see that I was wounded.

"How am I bleeding?" I asked anyone who could hear me, but I was completely alone.

8

FENTON

I sat on the edge of the bed with my head in my hands. Raine had tucked me into her roommate Troy's room and ordered me to rest while she, Loren, Javier, and Galinda talked about "what they were going to do." Which most likely meant, how they were going to kill Blaze Evanora and use his ex-wife to do it.

I needed a drink, or a pill, or to run twenty miles. Anything to make me feel something other than hopelessness.

My phone vibrated and I clicked silent. I couldn't talk to anyone right now. It was too much.

On a good day, I could answer the phone and remember it wasn't the enemy. Dad made his own decisions and me answering his call that day wouldn't have saved him. But today wasn't a good day, and today the phone taunted me with its vibrations.

My stomach grew tighter and tighter. Cold sweat trailed down the back of my neck. *Stop ringing*, I willed it. I covered my ears with my hands.

Having anxiety over a cell phone was ridiculous on the

surface; it was just a plastic and glass object filled with a small computer. It was nothing more than science. But it was a constant reminder of the one time I didn't answer. The one time I could have done something to save a life.

I always thought that if I lived a good life, if I treated all creatures with love and respect, they would treat me the same way. That was just my naivety. I couldn't understand how people could be so cruel, so hateful, but they were. It didn't matter if I was a vegan or a pacifist or spent my life denouncing that I was a hunter by birth.

The demons still came. They still tore my family apart. They still tore me apart.

As soon as the buzzing stopped, I scooped up my phone to turn it off. As I was powering down, it started ringing again. Hazel's name was scrawled across the screen. She had added herself into my phone after I started working at Billy's, but she knew only to text me.

So why was she calling?

I canceled the power down and declined her call before opening up a text message window.

Me: What?

Hazel: Answer UR damn phone

It started ringing again and nearly fell out of my sweaty palm, but I steadied myself with a deep breath and swiped a shaky finger across the screen to accept the call. It took me a solid five seconds to remember to lift it to my ear.

"Fenton!" Hazel whisper-shouted.

"S-sorry," I muttered, seemingly confused as how a phone operated. My head was swimming and my stomach rolled. My skin felt too tight and my bones too loose, and I clung to the phone with both hands. If I dropped it, I would never pick it up again.

"I'm going to be frank because I know you hate phones. Are you willing to risk dying for my sister?"

I nodded as if she could see me.

"Good. Me too," she replied as if she'd witnessed my acquiescence. "Tomorrow night we'll do the soul releasing spell."

Before I could say a word, I heard a door open and Grayson say something, and then the call ended.

Tomorrow night.

I could be dead tomorrow night and that sat better with me than killing someone.

My financial advisor knew what to do with my money, and Loren and Grayson could split the rest of my stuff between them. As a hunter, my body would be burned and then buried on sacred ground. Wow, that was my life sorted. Every decision, every indecision, every piece of pizza eaten and every five-mile run boiled down to these two things—who got my money and where I was buried.

I grabbed the remote and turned on the television, then dug into the snack stash Raine had put on the bedside table. Opening a bag of chips, I leaned back on the bed and flipped through the channels. I didn't have to worry about clogged arteries if I was going to die tomorrow. For the first time in several days, I smiled. Truly smiled.

I LOVED the six AM crowd at Eggs 'N Oinks, the local greasy spoon. There was a fairly even split between still-drunk college students and the above-seventy crowd who didn't take any shit. Mr. Anderson had sent his bacon back three times because it wasn't crispy enough and Claudia, who ran the dry cleaner, was on her fourth pass through the menu like she didn't eat here every day.

Even after a night of tossing and turning, my body was wide awake before the sunrise. Anticipation was burning a hole in my stomach. I was ready for a decision to be made and a plan of action to be enacted. Good or bad, this all ended tonight.

I was halfway through a surprisingly delicious order of vegan pancakes when my brothers walked in and made a beeline for my table. I soaked in every detail of Grayson's unshaven face and Loren's dark under eyes. I watched them play shove each other as they approached my booth. I tried to store the sound of their laughter to carry with me, just in case.

Loren reached over and grabbed my coffee mug, taking a big swig. I laughed at the face he made as he forced himself to swallow before grabbing my water and chugging half of it. "What?" I teased. "Don't like green tea?"

"It tastes like hedge clippings," he gasped, and then cleared his throat. "Why are we even up this early?"

I shrugged. "I wanted to watch the sunrise."

"It's November. The sun doesn't rise until like noon."

Grayson groaned at us to shut up and flagged down the waitress. "Nancy, two black coffees, two grapefruit juices, and two specials, one with bacon, one with sausage."

"You got it."

I raised my eyebrow. "You two are like the same person."

Loren pointed at me sternly. "Nope. I'm an all bacon guy. He likes putting sausage in his mouth."

Grayson shrugged. "Don't knock it until you try it."

I speared the last of my pancake with my fork and shoved the entire thing in my mouth. The two of them burst out laughing and for just one moment, everything was back the way it was, sitting around the kitchen table making fun of each other. I longed to go back to when everything was simple, when our parents were still alive, when every choice wasn't life and death.

We were silent until the food came, each presumably lost in our own morning thoughts.

Grayson held my gaze for a long moment before he looked down at his pancakes and cut off a chunk. "Hazel and I want to get a bigger place without shared walls." I scrunched up my face, but he ignored me. "She has another six months on her lease. If you're staying, would you like to sublet?"

How could I tell him it depended on if I survived the night? Of course, if I did, that would be way better than the motel. "That'd be awesome, man. Thanks."

He smiled. "Good. Because we signed the new lease yesterday and I already told Hazel you'd move in. We're moving next Monday."

"What if I said no?" *What if I can't because I'm dead?*

He grimaced. "I would've had to convince this guy" —he pointed to Loren— "and he and Raine are louder than—"

I held up my hand to stop him. "Yeah, yeah, I got it. I'm not banging anyone, so shared walls aren't an issue."

"Banging?" Loren asked, smirking.

"Not all of us have the vocabulary of a sailor when we're in public."

"What the fuck ever."

Grayson elbowed Loren. "Although, serious question, did you even put a door on Raine's room? Beaded curtains are not a good substitute. For real, I'll kick this asshole out"—he pointed at me— "and let you sublet instead."

Loren just stared at him. "I know where the hardware store is, thank you very much."

Grayson held up his fork and knife. "Easy there, killer. Just double checking."

"This is possibly the strangest conversation of my life," I muttered.

"Really? With 'Who Wore it Better: Thor or Wonder Woman' on the table?" Grayson quipped.

I point my fork at him. "You almost broke my nose. And obviously Wonder Woman."

He shrugged. "We were drunk. Anyway, she ain't got the shoulders. Thor all the way."

"We're not starting this again," Loren warned. "We agreed to disagree, remember?"

I sat back and sighed. "Well, thanks for helping me find a place. Let me know when I can help you move. I need to look at getting a truck this week, too."

Grayson pushed away his empty plate and pulled his coffee cup toward him, pushing the handle back and forth. "Are you sure you want to stay?"

I shrugged. "Whether I stay or not, I still need a truck."

"What happened to your old truck?"

I balled up and then smoothed out my straw wrapper. "Told my roommate to sell it to pay for me breaking my lease." After about fifty missed calls, he finally texted me and I told him to sell whatever he could. Everything important to me was in a safe deposit box back in Maine, near our childhood home.

"You were kidnapped," Grayson growled. "It's not like you purposefully left."

"I saw no reason to go back."

My brothers exchanged a look, then both focused on me. Grayson's eyes held mine. "We are concerned about what will happen should something happen to Romi."

We all heard what he really meant. *When something happens to Romi.*

I held up my hand to stop Grayson. I couldn't continue down this road, not today. "Tomorrow. We'll talk about it all tomorrow. As long as she's here and you both are here, I'm not planning on going anywhere." Technically not a lie.

"What happens if she's not here and we are? When we're on the sixth month of winter and endless gray skies?" Loren asked. "What then?" When I shrugged, he slammed his palm on the table. "You can't keep running, Fen. It wasn't your fault."

Standing, I pulled my wallet from my back pocket and tossed a few bills down to cover the bill and leave a good tip. "I'm off to the shelter."

Grayson winced and elbowed Loren. "Not cool, bro."

I turned on my heel and walked out the front door into the still-dark morning. It only took four steps for them to rush after me. They were never good at taking a hint.

"Fenton!" Loren called. I walked faster down the empty sidewalk, not turning around. "Goddamnit, Fenton, will you wait a minute?"

I didn't wait. They flanked me, forcing me to stop.

"What's your problem?" Loren barked.

"Nothing. You seem to know my mind better than I do. Romi will disappear, I'll get tired of winter, then bail. Just like you always do."

He shoved my shoulder. "I was working!"

I shrugged and made a sarcastic face. "Your job was more important than family. Got it."

"No. Saving people was more important."

"Until Raine, right?" By his flinch, I knew I hit a sore spot. "You can stick around for your girl and not your brothers. Well, guess what, I'm not like you. I wanted to stay around for the two of you, but I forgot how much you drive me fucking crazy."

"Stop being so dramatic. It's always your way or no way, right? God, you're just like Dad."

I threw the first punch, but he ducked out of the way.

Grayson stepped between us. I grabbed his hand and twisted it behind his back, making him lean into me or risk a broken arm. "Two years apart made me forget how annoying you both were!" he grumbled.

"You don't know anything about the last two years of my life. Don't pretend to." I let him go. Grayson and Loren just stared at me like I was a stranger. To them, I probably was.

"Then tell us," Loren said, finally. "What happened over the last two years?"

I stared at the horizon, the sun trying to crawl over the frosted tree line. An older couple passed us, and we all said good morning out of habit, but still didn't look at each other. I swallowed hard, deciding to just admit everything. After all, this could be my last day. The frigid wind slapped me across the face, as if telling me to spit it out and get it over with.

"I went to a party the night before Dad died," I admitted, watching how my breath came out like smoke and hung in front of me. A visible reminder that words were tangible things. "He wanted me to go with him on this hunt and we got into a big fight. I got really fucked up instead."

I shoved my hand in my hair and tugged at the curls, trying to keep my emotions in check. "He called me, before he died. He knew he was in trouble. I ignored the call. I ignored the last call he ever made. It's my fault he's dead and I've had to live with that guilt for two years."

I turned to Grayson. "So, no, I'm not the Fenton you knew before. And I never will be, again."

They were both silent for a long moment. Grayson grabbed my forearm. "Grief changes people, Fen. That's why we're trying to save Romi, no matter the cost. But we also understand if you can't stay here if we fail. I'm not sure I could if something happened to Hazel."

I nodded, but only because I needed to respond. I wouldn't be the same person tomorrow, whether or not I survived the spell tonight. He was right. Death changed people, even if it was only temporary—and especially if it was your own. I had listened to Raine's recount more than once. I knew her life would never be the same after her near brush with Hell.

Loren cleared his throat and looked down at his boots. "Dad's death wasn't your fault, just like Mom's death wasn't mine."

"No, that was the aneurysm," I retorted.

"No, it wasn't."

I took a step back, looking between my brothers. My stomach twisted with the foreshadowing of those three words. *It wasn't an aneurysm?* The delicious breakfast I had this morning turned into a rock in my stomach. I didn't need to be preternatural to know I wasn't going to like whatever Loren confessed.

From the confused look on Grayson's face, I could tell that he didn't know what Loren was talking about either. "What was it?" Grayson finally said the words I couldn't say.

Loren ran his palm over his buzzed head, looking over my shoulder at the rising sun. The air was cold, but the heat of anxiety prickled my skin. "Noiran had a partner. Zagos. She stalked Mom, Dad, and me after a trip that didn't go as planned."

Grayson took a step closer to me so we both faced Loren. Two against one. His jaw clenched and he swallowed hard before continuing. "Zagos followed me one night and attacked. She was about to kill me when Mom stepped in. Mom gave her life to save mine. Noiran was injured enough that he had to retreat."

I shook my head, unable to process what he has said. "A demon killed Mom?" I whispered. Loren sighed heavily and nodded. "Why didn't you tell us?"

"Dad asked me not to."

"He's been dead for two years!" I blinked hard and shook my head, trying to wrap my brain around this new information. "And Noiran?"

"Hell bent on revenge."

"You didn't think to tell us when Noiran came for a visit?"

"I was a little busy keeping my girlfriend and the town alive!"

My lungs refused to work, seized with the shock of the revelation. I hit my chest with my fist and gulped in air. The bitter wind picked up speed, and it sounded like roaring in my ears.

A demon killed my mother. And Loren had lied because of Dad, who was killed by a demon. I staggered a moment on my feet, the full circle like a knife to my chest. Was the purpose of this life only to hunt or be hunted?

"How could you not tell us?" Grayson asked so quietly I almost didn't hear him over the thudding of my heart.

Loren just shook his head. "Because you would've forgiven me, and I couldn't handle it." He looked right at me. "Sound familiar?"

Grayson, whose face had frozen in a dark mask of indifference, turned and walked away without saying a word. Loren watched him get in his truck and drive away, tires squealing. Following my middle brother's cue, I turned my back on Loren and walked away.

～

I HAD BEEN VOLUNTEERING at the animal shelter since I came to town. Loving animals but having a transient lifestyle made having a pet close to impossible. Even as I scooped near-frozen poop from the large, fenced-in yard out back, I still felt better when I was here. Especially today.

My head was still spinning from breakfast. I didn't want to be angry, not when my time was so short, but I didn't know how to forgive Loren for the years of lying, either. Once Dad was gone, why didn't he tell us? Or when Noiran came to town? Or when Raine laid down her powers and almost her life to save the people she loved?

I sucked in a huge lung full of winter air, letting the sting coat my throat, then blew it out slowly. Lenny, a beautiful golden retriever who really liked playing fetch, ran up to me with a soggy ball. He had some gray around his muzzle, but his eyes were still bright like a puppy's. "Hey boy," I said, and he wagged his tail harder. I was really going to miss him if I died.

Taking the disgusting ball from his mouth, I threw it across the yard and continued cleaning up as quickly as possible before my fingers went completely numb. The work gloves I was wearing were as much of a barrier from the cold as a tank top. It was on my third throw when I noticed Lenny didn't chase after the ball, but instead stood against my leg, growling. "Hey, Len, what's wrong?"

I followed his gaze but didn't see anything. I looked back and forth between the offending space and him before squatting down to rub his ears. "What do you see? Is it a squirrel?"

His ear ticked at the mention of his favorite animal, but his defensive position grew sharper. "There's nothing there," I tried, looking back over as if to show him. Except, now there was. The most pure black dog—or was it a wolf?—had appeared out of nowhere.

It growled unlike any animal I had ever heard. It sounded almost...human. I stood, keeping my eyes locked on the new dog. Sweat pricked the back of my neck, a warning that this wasn't an ordinary house pet. "Lenny, get inside."

He took a step backward and let out a bark but refused to leave my side. If I survived tonight, I needed to find out if Hazel's place was pet-friendly. He needed to come home with me immediately. He was such a good boy. "Len, let's go."

My steps were careful as I concentrated on not tripping or losing sight of the creature. When we reached the door, I fumbled for the handle. The creature took another step forward, eyes laser-focused, eyes that turned from dark to blazing red. He pulled his ears back and charged.

I grabbed Lenny and pulled us back into the building. The creature's bark pierced the morning like a chainsaw. I braced myself for an impact on the door, but none came. Breathing heavily, I looked down at Lenny, who had relaxed back into a goofy dog with his tongue hanging out of his mouth. A peek through the door's window confirmed that the yard was completely empty. "What the hell?" I whispered.

"Everything okay, Fenton?" Kendra, my supervisor, asked from the hallway. "I heard a door slam."

I turned to face her, confusion evident. "Do we have any all-black dogs? Like really big ones?"

She frowned and shook her head. "We have Tuxedo, who's black with white paws. But he's smaller than Lenny. Something happen?"

I gestured to the door. "There was a really aggressive dog hanging around the fence. Tried to attack Lenny." *Tried to attack me.* I didn't know what that thing was, but I had a feeling that I was the intended target, not the pup.

She walked over to the door and pushed it open, looking around the empty yard. "I'll have maintenance make sure the fence is intact. Mr. Harvey's herding dogs tend to sneak in every few months to create chaos. I'll call Marge at the station and let her know." She turned to walk away.

"Wait," I called. "I wanted to let you know that I won't be in tomorrow."

She looked up at me over the rim of her glasses.

"I..." *I, what, genius? May be dead? I'm on a mission to save my dead girlfriend?* "...have a family situation. Emergency."

She nodded. "Okay, thanks for letting me know. I hope everything is okay."

"Thanks."

As soon as she walked away, I pulled off my gloves and reached for my phone to text my brothers about the creature. Then the memories of this morning came crashing back. Letting the phone fall back into my pocket, I got back to work. I wasn't ready to talk to them yet, even about this.

Lenny happily followed me around for the rest of my shift. He seemed as reluctant to leave my side as I was to leave his. His presence comforted me in a way little else had in the last few years. I bent down and scratched him behind the ears. "I'll find a way to keep you, I promise." He let out a small bark and put his chin on my shoulder. "Good boy."

When my shift ended, I hovered by the door, not only because leaving Lenny behind was hard, but also because I really wished I had a car. It was a half mile back to the hotel and if there was a crazy demonic dog on the loose—and I was pretty sure that's what it was—I wanted to be protected by metal and glass. After looking around and not seeing anything but a few people moving in and out of the strip of stores, I took off at a dead run.

9

FENTON

I hadn't seen Romi in over twenty-four hours. It was the longest length of time since our first meeting and it was slowly destroying me. At eleven-thirty, I took a taxi to Hazel's apartment. The bridge that connected off-campus housing to the town was still out from the snowstorm, so we had to go the long way around town.

When I reached the parking lot, I pulled out my phone to text her. **Outside.**

Hazel: Be out in 5.

I tucked my phone back in my pocket and pulled my hood up, despite the fact that I was stress sweating beneath my hoodie. I hadn't bothered with a winter coat. Either this was going to work, or I'd be dead.

Something moved along the edge of the parking lot. Romi appeared for a single instant, a dark shadow holding a knife to her throat. Her eyes were wide, and her mouth was open on a silent scream.

Two men ran over to where she had been standing, one of them holding the small wooden box that was taken from my room. They turned red eyes to me.

Demons.

I shifted into a fighting stance. "You're not going to touch her," I shouted. I heard the apartment door open behind me and held up my hand. "Stay inside, Hazel." The door slammed shut and I knew she was going to wake Grayson. There was a protection spell on the building, and demons couldn't get inside, but spells were nearly impossible to keep in place outside. Weather and animals tended to erode protections.

The shorter demon opened the box while the other brandished a knife. I moved backward toward the apartment door. It swung open and Grayson and Hazel rushed out.

"They've got Romi. A demon or something, knife to her throat," I explained.

Grayson stood next to me, a shotgun with shells filled with salt in his hand. "Get back inside, Hazel! We got this," Grayson ordered.

"Not on your goddamn life!" she yelled back.

Grayson fired at the demons, hitting the one with the knife in the shoulder and the other in the shin. It shouldn't kill the humans if they were still alive, but it would really piss the demons off. Knife guy collapsed and the demon escaped his body on a cloud of smoke. But box guy didn't seem to care about his leg.

"Shoot me again and I'll give the kill order," he warned. "We wanted to take her soul to Hell, have a little fun with her. But I have no problem just eviscerating her."

Hazel looked over her shoulder. "Now or never, Fenton."

"This seems like a really inopportune time," I responded.

Grayson's shoulders stiffened, but he didn't turn around. "Inopportune time for what?"

63

"Something you're not going to like," Hazel said. She pulled a Post-it note from her pocket and flattened it in her palm. "I need you to get the candle and lighter from my other pocket and light it. Don't let them see."

"Absolutely not going to happen!" Grayson snapped.

"So you'll let my sister's soul be eviscerated for all eternity, even after your brother volunteered to risk his life to save her?" she shot back.

A growl to my left made my stomach drop. Four dogs, dark as night with blood-colored eyes, came out of the shadows. "Well, this isn't great," I said.

They started to run toward us, and I knew we missed our chance. Already snapping their jaws, we were dead if they reached us. Grayson fired another shot, then another, but the creatures didn't even slow.

I reached over and gripped Grayson's hand. "You and Loren were the best fucking brothers a guy could have. I love you. I hope this works." Then I started running toward the demon, waving my hands in the air to distract the dogs. "GET INSIDE NOW!" I ordered.

One dog jumped onto the demon, pushing him to the ground. The demon poured out of the human, then the dog and the shadow circled each other. I couldn't tell if they were fighting or playing, and didn't have time to care.

I cut out of the parking lot and headed toward the bridge. The giant chasm was still there from the storm. If I could leap across and the demon dogs fell, it would probably give us enough time to do the spell. If not, well, that was going to suck.

I felt the zing right before Romi appeared next to me, limping more than running. "I'm here, Fen. I got away. I'm here with you."

She reached out and grabbed my hand. I couldn't feel

the pressure of her grip, just the coldness of her pulling on my energy. We jumped over the orange cones and ran around the construction sign.

We ran harder, faster, and at the count of three jumped. I lost contact with her hand as two of the dogs jumped with us, capturing us with their jaws. There was a flash of indescribable pain, and then I fell into darkness.

10

ROMI

W hen I opened my eyes, I was on the floor of my childhood kitchen. I looked to the left, seeing the chewed corner of the candy-apple red cabinets. My dog, Gus, used to bite there when he was nervous. I missed him terribly.

With a groan, I forced myself up on my elbows. "Fenton? Where are you? Are you okay?"

Silence...no, not silence. Negative sound.

Fear permeated the air as I gripped the edge of the dark granite countertop and struggled to pull myself up. Everything hurt, just like it had when Natalia stabbed me, like it had when the hellhounds had sunk their teeth into my body.

Like in Hell.

"FENTON!" I screamed, running toward the front door, trying to pull it open. "You can escape," I told myself. "Focus. Don't think about anything else."

My body was forced backward and to the stove, where a cast-iron Dutch oven appeared on the gas burner. A timer went off and I started moving on autopilot. "No, *please* no!" I cried, but my body was no longer in my control. I grabbed tongs and pulled the vegetables off the grill.

Romi, focus. What did I need to do? I'm forgetting something.

As I pulled the chicken out of the Dutch oven, Mom came through the front door and threw her keys into the dish on the entry table. Gus, our black lab, scurried over to greet her as if she'd been gone for a month instead of nine hours.

What was I just thinking about? Oh good, Mom's home.

"Did you make dinner?" she asked me. "What did I do to deserve you?"

"Yep! Went with that chicken recipe you both liked."

She walked over and kissed my cheek. "Perfect. Your dad should be home any minute."

By the time Dad walked in, Mom had reappeared from changing her clothes and I had plated the food. Dad washed his hands and leaned against the sink. "Where's your other half?"

I closed an eye, trying to think. "I think she said she was going to the movies with her boyfriend? She told me while I was making my grocery list, so I really wasn't paying attention."

He raised an eyebrow. "That was an amateur move."

"Right?" I laughed.

He looked over at Mom. "She's only sixteen. Is she allowed to have a boyfriend?"

Mom rolled her eyes. "Like you didn't have a girlfriend by thirteen?"

Dad winced. "Great. My daughter's turning out just like me." He walked over to the television and flipped on the news.

"Why are you going to ruin my delicious meal with that?" I crossed my arms and gave him a mock glare.

"Just the first fifteen minutes, I promise. And I'll mute it." He shook the remote at me, then set it on the table.

I rolled my eyes at the same old argument we had every night, then followed him and my mom to the table. Gus laid down next to my feet, just in case I dropped a tasty morsel on the floor. After serving my parents, I filled my own plate.

Mom swallowed then looked at me. "This tastes different. Not bad, just different than I remember."

I shoved a forkful in my mouth and chewed thoughtfully. I had bought the same ingredients. The same chicken, the same oil, the same breadcrumbs. Somehow this batch had a new flavor; a nutty flavor. My fork fell to the table. "DAD! STOP!" I screamed, jumping out of my seat and racing around the table to knock the fork out of his hand.

But it was too late.

His hand was at his throat as he gasped for air. Mom ran for the epinephrine pens and I dialed 9-1-1 as he slumped forward, his lips already blue. Gus barked over and over again at the commotion. Mom shoved the pens into Dad's leg, but he didn't move. The doctor had warned us that his nut allergy had gotten so severe that the pens may not work anymore.

"MOM!" I screamed, tears mixing with snot on my face. "WE HAVE TO DO SOMETHING!" The emergency operator was speaking, but I let my phone fall to the table.

I ran into my dad's office and pulled some bobby pins from my hair, jamming them into the lock on the main drawer until the latch released. I pulled out the cracked leather book and onyx candle wrapped in cloth. The scent of linen and roses—my grandma's perfume—wafted around me.

My grandmother had practiced dark magic until the day she died, then left these artifacts to her son in her will. She told Dad one day he'd need them. I had popped open this drawer so many times after her death just to feel close to her again. Now, my ability to pick a lock was going to save a life. It had to.

Mom shook her head when I walked back in, her fingers resting on Dad's pulse point. I flinched then shook my head. I refused to let him die.

I shoved the candle at her and flipped open the book to the spell to bring a newly dead person back to life. The doorbell rang and I heard the first responders yell.

"Mom, light the candle. Now!"

She went to the gas stove and turned on a burner, then lit the wick. The very air shimmered around the flame. The responders yelled again, trying to open the door. I grabbed a knife from the table, piercing my thumb.

My mom held out the candle and I grabbed it, pressing my blood into the wax-like substance, making the blood oath that I would give up whatever the spell cost. She wrapped her hand around mine and held up the book.

We read the spell that would bring my dad back to life. When we had reached the end, the candle blew out on its own. The first responders shoved through the door the moment my dad took a deep breath.

He turned his head to look at me, but his purple eyes were gone. In their place were completely black irises. Then, in a blink, they turned to blue.

I closed the book and shoved it behind my back as the team approached Dad to take his vitals. Even with the book behind me, I could still see the warning on the next page, scrawled in Grandma's hand. Devil magic came at the highest price. A life for a life.

I closed my eyes and took a deep breath as nausea washed over me. When I opened them again, I was at the stove. As I pulled the vegetables off the grill and the chicken out of the Dutch oven, Mom came through the front door and threw her keys into the dish on the entry table. Gus, our black lab, scurried over to greet her.

11

FENTON

The ringing of a phone woke me up.

"Romi?" My head throbbed with each heartbeat, pain radiating from the top of my head and spreading all the way down my spine. "You here or did you have another nightmare? I think I'm having them, too."

Nausea rolled around my stomach and I groaned, turning onto my back and rubbing my temples. I needed to get something for this migraine before it got any worse.

I reached over to the nightstand but couldn't find the phone. *Where had I left my cell?*

Slowly, I squinted my right eye open against the brightness of the room. The winter sun seeped in through the window of my bedroom, making the blue walls look gray.

Frowning, I pushed myself up on my elbows and looked around. *Why was I on the floor?* The family photo of my brothers and our parents was hanging sideways on the wall, a crack splintering the glass. Next to the photo was a hole in the drywall that looked like someone had punched it.

A chill ran down my spine. This wasn't Hayvenwood Motel. This was my bedroom back in Maine. "Hello? Romi?"

Silence answered me.

Pushing myself to my feet, I walked over to the picture and traced the frame. That was the very last time we were all together. My favorite picture. *Why was I here? How did I get here?*

"Hello?" I called again, but I couldn't remember who I was looking for. The pain in my head throbbed so hard, my vision blurred. I stumbled to the dresser where a bottle of ibuprofen rested. I choked down two and crawled to my bed, burying myself in the blankets.

Why did I feel like shit? Did I drink too much last night? Was this the flu? Did I work today? Where was my cell?

Lifting my head reluctantly off the pillow, I spotted my cellphone on the nightstand next to my wallet. Good. I hadn't lost them.

With a sigh, I pulled the pillow over my head and closed my eyes. I was just drifting off to sleep when the phone started ringing. "Go away!" I groaned, my head giving me a vicious kick for daring to speak.

Finally, the ringing stopped, but it started up again right away. Fumbling for the phone, I rejected the call and turned it off, then threw it across the room. Sleep crept up again until a staticky voicemail started playing, the harsh, hurried whisper of the caller echoed around the room.

"It's Dad. You didn't show up, Fen. I need you. They've got me cornered. Please hurry. I texted my location. Love you. I—" His sentence cut off with a guttural scream, the pain in his voice so potent, I leaned over the edge of the bed and threw up onto my floor.

I scrambled out of bed, trying to reach my cell phone. My feet took the steps, but I didn't move forward. The voicemail started playing over and over again, getting louder and louder until it was ear-splitting. "Dad! I'm coming, Dad!

Hold on!" I screamed, guilt and pain clogging my chest and filling my lungs.

But my feet wouldn't move, and the voicemail wouldn't stop playing. Over and over and over again. Then my body started moving on its own, dragging me over to the wall. My arm drew back, and I punched the drywall. My fist made a hole and cracked the glass in the frame.

Still, the voicemail played on.

I fell to my knees and covered my ears. "Please stop!" I begged. "Please, please, please. I'm sorry, Dad, I'm so sorry. I'm the reason he's dead." A sob ripped through my chest, threatening to break my ribs. "It's my fault."

The voicemail stopped and the room grew dim. I laid back down on the floor and welcomed sleep. I just needed some sleep for this headache.

My body stilled and I closed my eyes. Then a phone started ringing and I squinted one eye open.

Where had I left my cell? Slowly, I squinted my right eye open against the brightness of the room. The winter sun seeped in through the window of my bedroom, making the blue walls look gray.

12

ROMI

For one brief moment, my mind grasped that I was in Hell, that I was locked in a room and the memory of killing my father just looped over and over again. *Put the plates down. Take a bite. Run for the book. Light the candle. Wake Dad. Sell my soul.*

Over and over again, the scene repeated. I killed my father once, twice, two hundred, three thousand times. *How did I escape before? Didn't I escape? Where was I? Had I always been here?*

As I plated the food, a woman with dark hair and ice-blue eyes walked in the front door and stared. She looked familiar and I opened my mouth to ask her why she was here, but couldn't stop the pull to walk toward the table, holding the deadly chicken. She cried silently as she watched me kill my father two more times.

When I closed the book behind my back, the woman stepped forward and lifted up the television remote, then unmuted the television. The newscaster's voice filtered through the chaos. "In national news today, there's been a recall on Farmer Smith's Breadcrumbs because of an accidental cross-contamination with crushed almonds..."

The scene reset, but everything blinked in and out once, like poor television reception. The woman stood next to the table and grabbed the remote, turning on the television as Mom walked in the door. She turned it up so loud, I couldn't hear the conversation between my parents.

The woman walked over to the counter and pushed the breadcrumbs into my hand. I looked down at them as I walked toward the table. Farmer Smith's Breadcrumbs. "Who are you?" I asked, but I couldn't hear her response.

We sat down and cut the chicken. The newscaster on the television said something about Farmer Smith's Breadcrumbs, and I looked at the container just before I saw Dad's lips turn blue. *It wasn't your fault*, a small voice said. I didn't know if it was in my head, or the beautiful woman standing next to me, but time slowed until it was nearly frozen.

Half of me started to move forward, but a shadow of myself reached over and picked up the container, flipping it over to study the ingredients. "Bread crumbs." There were no nuts listed.

Cross-contamination...

"I didn't kill him," I said out loud. "I didn't kill him!" My shoulders felt lighter, as self-forgiveness took hold deep inside me. The woman pressed a hand to her chest in visible relief. The scene around me didn't end, it just changed. I was pulled into the study, where I was picking open the drawer and grabbing the journal.

I was still the one who had grabbed the spell-book. I was still the one that forced my mom to read, giving her the first hit of such an addictive drug. Again and again, the second half of the memory played out, even as I fought against the pull.

The beautiful woman—and the sense of déjà vu that came with her—ran through the scene, pulling things out of drawers, going through bags, and lifting up couch cushions. After three more rotations, I found her searching the bottom of the trash can. She emerged with two dark sticks in her hand and ran over to hold them in front of me.

In her palms lay the stubs of two dark magic candles, already burned.

This wasn't the first dark magic used in the house.

"It wasn't your fault," the woman whispered. "You didn't kill your dad, and you're not the reason they started using dark magic."

I stared at her, letting the words sink in. *It's not my fault.* "It's not my fault," I whispered.

My house disintegrated, the colorful kitchen revealing a dust-filled cavern. My parents were no more than shadows that evaporated, and with a whimper, my dog was gone.

Hands grabbed my upper arms, and I turned to find Laura Lynch staring back at me. She was the beautiful woman I hadn't recognized when I was lost in my guilt. "You came for me. How'd you escape your cell?"

The look on her face broke my heart. "I don't know. I was reliving..." she cleared her throat. "I heard my son's voice and it somehow pierced the cycle. I ran to the door and saw them throw him in a room. I wanted to go get him, but I was afraid to go in by myself. If we both got stuck, I couldn't help him."

She gripped my shoulders. "I knew you'd be here. I knew you wouldn't let him come to Hell alone."

I shook my head. "Never."

She gave me a quick hug. "Hurry, we need to save my son."

13

ROMI

Laura grabbed my hand and ran ahead of me, pulling me out the door and around a corner. I froze as a dozen separate hallways spread out in front of us. Screams and tears and mocking laughter filled the spaces between each room.

She tugged me and stepped forward confidently down a hallway to the left of us.

I stumbled, but easily righted myself. "How do you know where he is?"

Something dark flew overhead, so close that my hair shivered. I hunched forward but kept running as it circled back. "Laura!"

She watched the shadow swoop in again and yanked me against the side of the door, holding her finger to her lips. The thing bolted past us, twisting like smoke. *Demon.*

She squeezed my hand, and I reveled in the feel of it. With only a nod for warning, we set out again, our steps quick and whisper quiet. Laura was counting under her breath, and I realized she must know the number of steps it took to get to the cell. Smart thinking; this place was a labyrinth.

We slowed and then stopped in front of a white bedroom door, decorated with pictures of Laura's family and their pets. She didn't need to confirm out loud that this was our destination. I could tell by the slump of her shoulders and the desperate look in her eyes, as well as the photos of teenage Fenton with friends I'd probably never meet.

"I don't know if I can go in and not get trapped," she admitted. "He's part of my guilt cycle."

I looked between her and the door. "What do I do? How do I save him?"

She turned to face me and took both my hands in hers. "You need to make him see it wasn't his fault. The moment you break the cycle, he'll be free."

I nodded. "Okay." I gave her a quick hug.

"Hurry," she whispered. "He may still be alive."

Without wasting another moment, I pushed into his room.

It was clear he didn't recognize me, even though his eyes met mine for a brief moment. This must be a trick of the cell. I stood frozen in horror as I watched the scene unfold once, then again trying to find a loophole.

I didn't know what to say to him, what to do to release him from his guilt. There was no other context, no other people. Just him and the cellphone. His father's death was Noiran's fault, no matter what choices Fenton made. In fact, Fenton would've most likely died had he gone with his father.

And he was going to die now if I didn't get him out of this cell.

His skin was ghost white, except for the dark circles

under his unfocused eyes. Healed bite marks covered his neck and arms, and I physically ached at the thought of teeth piercing his skin. I had no idea how long he'd been trapped here, but the sharpness of his bones and the strain permanently marring the space between his eyebrows terrified me. I walked up to him and wrapped my arms around his waist, but it was like I wasn't even there.

"Fenton! Come on, look at me. It's me. It's Romi. Come on." I shook his shoulders, but he walked around me, never blinking. I followed him and stepped in front of him again. "I'm so sorry," I whispered just before I slapped him as hard as I could across the face.

He flinched, but his eyes didn't meet mine. He seemed completely unaware of my presence. I looked around, trying to figure out how to physically drag him out of here. He was significantly bigger than me, but I was solid in Hell.

Grabbing the top sheet off the bed, I twisted it until it made a rope, then wrapped the ends around my hands. The scene reset and the sheet reappeared on the bed, but I got faster. It reset again and again, until I could make the temporary restraint in a matter of seconds.

Grab. Twist. Wrap.

This time I walked up to Fenton and twisted it around his ankles. I pushed him over and started dragging him to the door. I didn't make it very far before the scene reset again. "Dammit!" I sobbed. "Why couldn't you have a longer guilt trip?"

His breathing was growing shallow and I knew we were running out of time. "I'm not going to let you die," I promised. "I can't."

I tried his mid-section, his wrists, behind his knees, but even in his weakened form, he was stronger than me. I crawled to the cell door and pushed through it. Laura's radiant smile fell the moment she realized I was alone. "I'm sorry," I whispered, then broke down crying.

I didn't even know I could cry in Hell. She wrapped her shaking arms around me. "Let's get Genevieve. She can help." We both ignored the way her voice cracked.

I shook my head. "If we don't get him out now, we're going to lose him." I searched her face. "What if we blindfold you? I just need you to help me pull him out. I'm not strong enough."

She shook her head and her eyes filled with tears, but she said, "Anything for my son." She started to tremble. She shrugged out of the thin sweater she was wearing and fashioned it into a blindfold, folding it into several layers before making a knot at the back of her head. "Okay, I'm ready."

I took her hand and opened the door, guiding her inside. "Stay here. Don't move until I tell you to." I went to work as soon as the scene reset, grabbing the sheet and making my impromptu lasso. As soon as I had him tied up, I put some of the sheet in Laura's hand. "Pull as hard as you can!"

We both pulled hard, making it halfway to the door. I swore when everything started over. "We need to go faster!" Again, then again, we tried until my arms were screaming in protest. Fenton was still fighting back, forced to relive the movements that trapped him here. This arm caught, that leg kicked, and the timing was impossible.

Tears stung my eyes. I was failing him. "Laura, I don't know what to do," I whispered.

She stood very still for a long moment, then pulled the blindfold off her face and squeezed her eyes shut. "Blindfold him."

"Don't open your eyes."

"HURRY!"

I grabbed the sweater from her hand and wrapped the sweater around his face. He fought back and slammed us into the wall, causing a picture frame to hit him in the head. He sank down to the ground.

"Come back to me," I ordered. He lay completely still for one rotation, then two.

I shook his shoulder once, then again, but he was completely unresponsive. "Fenton, come on love, I need you to get up." I tried not to let panic creep into my voice. "Come on, babe. We need to get out of here." I wrapped myself around him and tried to pull him up, but we both collapsed. "Laura, I need you to help me."

She nodded and walked forward, hands extended out. "Guide me."

"Six steps forward...good. Now go to your left four..." Carefully, and oh so slowly, she made her way over to her son's body. She took his legs and I lifted him under the shoulders. "Back up slowly. One more step. Good."

We were only a few feet from the door when Laura stumbled and went down. Fenton fell to the side and I toppled on top of him. "You okay, Laura?" I asked as I scrambled upright and resumed my hold on Fenton.

She didn't answer me. Instead, she stood and walked back into the room, her eyes wide open. I looked behind me and the scene had changed. This time, she was standing in a field with her husband and a very young Loren, facing off with a creature that looked human but had scales down its arms.

"Fuck!" I screamed. "Laura, come back. Please! Your son needs you!"

She shook her head. "It's my fault. If we hadn't forced

Lucian to hunt so young, we wouldn't have angered the demons. My husband, my friends, Genevieve. We'd all still be alive if I hadn't made him make that first kill." She started crying. "I was a terrible mother."

Laura went over to Loren and then helped him raise the gun. "Shoot it," she ordered.

"Please don't kill me!" the creature screamed. "I have a family, just like you."

Loren hesitated.

The creature tried to grab the gun, but Laura reached out and took it back, then twisted the creature's arm until there was a sickening snap. "SHOOT NOW!" she ordered.

Young Loren, who looked no more than six, was sobbing as he pulled the trigger. The creature fell to the ground in a heap.

With another expletive, I lowered Fenton to the ground and walked around to his ankles. Inch by inch, I pulled Fenton toward the entrance as I watched Laura relive her memory.

When I finally reached the door, I shoved it open and tried not to let it close on important things, like ribs and heads.

It took the last of my energy to prop Fenton up against the wall outside his cell. I slipped his blindfold off and pressed my fingers to his pulse. It was weak but steady. I looked back at the door before I closed it, my heart screaming to go in and save Laura.

Laura was dead and the cell wouldn't kill her, but if I didn't get Fenton out of here, he would die. "I'm sorry, I'm so sorry," I said as I closed her inside. She escaped once. Hopefully she could escape again.

I looked around, trying to find anything that could help me drag a body out of here. I went to the next cell, then the next, trying to find a wagon or a wheelchair or something. I hadn't tried to take anything out of a room before, but if I did it before it reset, maybe I could manage it. I kept my eyes to the floor, not looking at the people or the playback of their guilt. I couldn't stand it and I didn't have time to help them.

Finally, sixteen doors later, I found a wagon that appeared abandoned in an overgrown backyard. I grabbed it and ran to the door, tumbling over the threshold with just moments to spare. I waited outside as the screaming started, then faded, then again waited through the entire story. The wagon stayed solid.

Convinced it wasn't going to disappear on me, I ran toward Fenton. I turned the wagon sideways and draped him over it, then I pushed it upright. He lay across it awkwardly, but he was in it and we were mobile.

Grabbing the handle, I ran down the corridor the way we had come. I tripped and fell, hit my legs with the wagon, and bloodied my knees, but I didn't slow. We needed to get out of the tangled web of cells and to a portal. I knew there was one near my door, because I had escaped once before, shortly after my death.

I took a corner too fast and the wagon tilted, dumping Fenton on the ground. I swore and fought back the urge to cry and I struggled to get him back on the wagon. Wiping my tears away with my sleeve, I looked around trying to figure out how to escape. I took two steps forward, then stopped as I passed Fenton's door again.

There was no way I ran in a circle. This was a trick from Hell. A sob burst through my chest and I covered my face with my sleeve. Fenton stirred and I stilled, then kneeled down next to him.

I took his head in my hand and kissed him softly. "Fenton, I need you to wake up." I shook his shoulders and kissed him again, reveling in the feel of his lips against mine. He shifted in the wagon, then blinked up at me. "Angel," he whispered. "What's wrong? Where are we?"

14

Every inch of my body was on *fire*. My blood had somehow turned to molten lava and each laborious beat of my heart was pure agony. I blinked hard and my vision cleared. Romi stood in front of me, cradling my head in her hands.

Her palms were like ice, an oasis in this fever dream. "Romi," I whispered. "What's going on?" I struggled to push myself out of the child's wagon, wincing at the ache in my knees. Did someone hit me with a baseball bat repeatedly? She motioned for me to stay seated, but at least I was upright.

"We're in Hell, Fen. We took the hellhounds with us when we jumped."

"I'm dead?" I gasped, then pressed two fingers to my pulse point. I still had a galloping heartbeat.

She shook her head. "No, not yet. Honestly, I don't even know how you're awake..." She searched my face for a long moment, as if she could read something there.

"I heard your voice," I admitted. "I needed to see you. I was so worried." My head was swimming and it felt like I was underwater so deep, my chest was going to cave in, but I was awake. *Deep breath. Focus.*

Romi looked over her shoulder at a door that was identical to the bedroom door I had growing up. "In Hell, you're forced to relive the moment you regret the most, the one you feel the most guilt over until you forgive yourself. Your mom saved me and then we saved you. But now she's trapped, and I can't help her alone."

"My mom?" The words were barely audible.

She nodded. "She and Genevieve are trapped. Just like they were in my dreams."

Adrenaline surged through me. "They weren't nightmares, they were real?" She nodded. I pushed myself upright and stumbled out of the wagon. "Let's go!" I gripped her wrist and pulled her toward the cell.

"Wait!" She tugged back. "I need to blindfold you. You won't survive if you get trapped again."

I released her wrist and we both turned back to where the wagon was, but it had disappeared. "No…" She looked around frantically. "No! Where is it? Where's the wagon?"

I turned in a circle, searching the hallway, but it was gone. She caught my elbow as I weaved on my feet. Releasing a slow breath, I steadied myself. Meeting her eyes, I saw the truth reflected back in them. We were running out of time. "What do we do?"

"You did not kill your father."

I blinked, trying to focus on her face. "Romi—"

She shook me slightly. "Listen to me. You *have* to believe me before we walk into that room, or we'll never save your mother. You didn't kill your father, you are not responsible for his death. Okay, so you didn't meet him, but he still chose to go on the mission. Noiran was always going to win that fight. You saw firsthand how strong he was."

She cradled my face in her hands. "Say it and mean it. 'I didn't kill my father. It's not my fault.'"

Maybe it was the fact that I knew I was dying, or that some part of my subconscious remembered being trapped in that cell, but her words penetrated all my shields and shame. Closing my eyes, I tried to absorb them and hold them close. "I didn't kill my father," I whispered.

"It's not my fault," she prompted.

Swallowing hard, I blew out a breath and let the words roll around in my mouth for a moment, letting truth stick to the edges. "It's not my fault."

"Again."

"I didn't kill my father. It's not my fault."

She gave me a soft kiss. "I'm proud of you." Her palms tapped on my cheeks in reassurance before pulling back. "Now or never. Keep your eyes closed as long as possible. We're going to go in, we'll grab her, and just run like hell. Got it?"

I nodded. "Let's do it." I reached for her hand and she twined her fingers through mine. She put her hand over my eyes and gently brushed down my eyelids.

As soon as we moved through the threshold, the air changed. It was an electric charge, the moments before a lightning strike. Each step was heavy, each breath harder. An invisible force tugged on my memories, trying to call forth the night Dad died.

I didn't kill my father. It's not my fault. I repeated the mantra over and over again as Romi guided me. My eyes started to open, and I threw my hand over them. Romi's hand went over mine as I heard my mom scream.

"We are right next to her," Romi said. "I'll guide your arms and you grab her securely."

I nodded, it sounded like a solid plan. Until I heard my

mom—the one only a few feet away—cry out. "I'm sorry! I'm so sorry, my sweet boy. I was a terrible mother."

My heart broke inside of my chest. "No, you were a wonderful mother." An unexpected sob caught me off guard and I dropped my hand, taking Romi's with it. I opened my eyes with determination and walked toward my mom. Fuck Hell if it was going to make her feel guilty for being an incredible Mom.

Romi gasped, but stepped back, trusting me. I walked right through the scene and grabbed my mom from behind. "YOU WERE A WONDERFUL MOTHER!" I yelled so loud the scene filled with static.

Mom tried to resist my hold, her arms and feet kicking and slapping, but my need to protect her was stronger. The adrenaline pumping through my veins overrode my exhaustion and dehydration. I was going to save her just like she had saved me over and over again since the day I was born.

Romi ran ahead and opened the door and I barreled through and into the passageway. I held onto Mom while she reoriented herself and regained her balance. Then she turned around to face me, tears overflowing from her eyes.

"My Rune," she said quietly, using my hunter name. "My strongest boy." She wrapped her arms around me and hugged me so tight, it almost hurt. I soaked in every inch of the mom-hug, knowing that they were in limited supply.

She pulled her left arm away and gestured for Romi to join us. After one more hug, we all took a step back, although Mom kept her arm around my waist. Romi and Mom had a silent conversation before Romi nodded. "Lead the way to Genevieve, then let's get out of here."

With Mom's steadying arm across my waist and Romi's hand in mine, we made our way through the maze. Mom counted the steps, repeating small phrases to help her with directions. As the adrenaline wore off, my head started swimming.

Each breath was forced, each step left me more off balance. My heart felt like it was doing a marathon in my parched throat. Jaw clenched, I focused on taking one step and then another. I didn't want to miss a moment with my mom.

There was no hesitation when we reached the frosted glass door to Genevieve's cell. It was beautiful and ornate, standing guard to a stone porch surrounded by planters full of summer flowers. The three of us walked in on Raine playing a baby grand piano in the living room. Genevieve sat next to her, apologizing over and over again for something I couldn't make out.

Romi pulled the blanket off the back of the couch and a water bottle off the side table. Mom and I physically grabbed Genevieve and pulled her out of the room. She kicked and writhed, screaming that she couldn't leave her daughter.

"I'm so sorry, Raine! I'm so sorry!" she screamed. "I can't leave my daughter!"

As soon as we dragged her over the threshold, her body went limp. Mom scooped her up in a hug and held her tight as they both cried. Romi pushed the water bottle in my hand and told me to drink.

"You first," I choked out.

She smiled and shook her head. "We're all dead. Drink."

Without hesitation, I downed the entire bottle, the contents not nearly enough to quench my undying thirst. I blinked sandpaper eyelids as the ground swam in front of me.

"We need to go, now," Mom said, then set a brisk pace.

As we passed a perfectly still pool of water, Romi pointed. "I went through the water before. Can we jump?"

Mom shook her head. "We can't risk him drowning. We need an above ground portal."

The farther we went, the weaker I became. My knees grew numb until they could barely support me. It was too hard to hold up my head, and I let my chin sink to my chest. I just needed to rest, just for a moment.

"Fenton, stay with me!" Romi cried as I sank to the ground.

Then everything went black.

15

ROMI

I had never felt more helpless than when Fenton passed out in front of me. I wrapped my arms around his shoulders, supporting his head before it hit the ground. Laura took the blanket off my shoulder and spread it out. "Roll him onto this. We'll carry him."

With the efficiency only two mothers could produce, we were moving with the blanket between us only seconds later. In an unspoken agreement, we were practically sprinting, no longer worried about tiring Fenton out. Now, we needed to get him back to the human world before it was too late.

"Left!" Laura called. "Then we're there!"

As we rounded the corner, the cave's opening loomed in front of us. "There's no way they're going to let us just walk out of here," I warned.

As if waiting for their cue, a pack of hellhounds walked into the quickly diminishing space between us and the exit. We slowed but didn't stop, playing chicken with the hounds. "Any ideas?" Laura asked.

Genevieve nodded. "Can you two carry him?"

"Yes, why?" Laura asked.

Genevieve handed her corner of the blanket to Laura. "Because I'm about to issue a really big thank you for rescuing me." She ran around me, then went full speed toward the dogs, yelling and screaming and waving her arms.

They took off after her as she pulled them away from the cave entrance and into the desert that waited beyond. When we reached the threshold, Laura pointed to a shimmering half-circle, guarded by a demon. "There. We need to get through the guard and we're home free."

Genevieve was running back toward us, only one hell-hound still chasing her. "GO!" she shouted.

"I'll make sure she gets out," Laura promised, although I heard the worry in her tone.

As we took a step into the blinding brightness—although there was no sun, so I had no idea how it was so bright—the hellhound knocked Genevieve to the ground and sank its jaws into the back of her neck.

Grabbing the other end of the blanket, I turned away from the attack. "Let's move."

"Wait!" she cried, tilting her head toward the portal. "Demons."

I followed her line of sight to the group of shadows lined up in front of the shimmery curtain. My chest burned with the desire to take each and every one of them out. "I'm so tired of fucking demons," I muttered.

Genevieve let out a small scream and our heads both turned in her direction. "I'm going to get her," I told Laura. "If you see an opening, run." I bolted out of the cave, feet pounding. Pulling out my demon-fighting moves, I jumped on its back and pulled it away from Genevieve. Thankfully, with her being a spirit, there was no blood. Just probably an insane amount of pain.

After a few kicks and some sand in its eye, the demon dog whimpered and slinked away, tired of this game. "Come on, Genevieve, I need you to wake up!" I rolled her over and put my hands under her armpits. "Eyes open. Help me out."

She didn't respond. Hell was for the birds. Thankfully, she was lighter than Fenton, maybe that whole spirit thing, and we were making our way back to the cave undetected.

Laura was motioning for me to hurry as she moved along the outer wall, inching toward the portal. "Is she dead?" she asked, looking over her friend.

I raised an eyebrow. "I mean, she was already dead. She can't die again." I blew my hair out of my face.

Laura's hand squeezed my shoulder. "Let's get them both on the blanket and then pull."

"What about the demons?"

She gestured to the portal. "One goes through every thirty seconds or so—theoretically, I'm just counting out loud. By the time we get there, we should only have the guard to deal with."

Following her instructions, we rearranged the blanket then waited until the last demon was about to go through the portal. "Charge and run through?" I asked.

"Absolutely a solid plan," Laura said.

We took off running, as fast as we could while pulling two people on a blanket. As we neared, the guard, who was not quite human-shaped, grew three times his size to block our path. No light reflected on him, as if it were made of a negative space. He spoke in words that sounded like many languages simultaneously, but somehow I still understood.

"The one with the heartbeat can go through." The guard turned in Laura and Genevieve's direction. "You aren't supposed to be here." We took a step forward, but the guard put up its hand. "Not you," it said to me.

"We're not leaving without her. She's not supposed to be here, either," Laura ordered in her most threatening mom-voice.

The demon shrank back for a moment. Apparently, even demons were a little bit afraid of Laura Lynch. This didn't surprise me; she was even more formidable in death, I suspected.

"I cannot allow her to go through," the demon responded after a long pause. "She is the result of dark magic. Unless the curse is broken, she cannot leave."

I looked down at Fenton. His skin was ashen and he had stopped sweating, which was a bad sign. I pressed my fingers into his neck to find his pulse, which was so weak I could barely count the beats. I was officially out of time.

Laura read the panic on my face. "Rosemary, what?"

"We're out of time. You have to take him through." I looked at her, desperate.

She nodded. "I'll take him and come back for you and Genevieve."

"No re-entry." The look she gave the demon even scared me a little.

I turned to her. "Two choices. Leave Genevieve and we'll go through the portal in the water. Or, if you can manage it, you go through with them both now. It's not far. You just have to make it through the door, okay?" I had no idea if that was true, but hope was a powerful thing. She needed to believe she could do it.

She shook her head. "I can't leave you."

I forced myself to smile reassuringly. "I'll find a way. I promise." It was either what she needed to hear, or my lying skills were getting better. I took the blanket from her hand

and I made two large knots to act as handles, and then handed them to Laura. "You need to go. Now."

She wrapped me in a fierce hug and kissed my forehead. "I'll get a message to Hazel, somehow. Tell her you're alright."

"Thank you," I whispered.

I helped her drag the blanket to the opening, my hands on hers. The guard flashed in front of me, blocking my exit. "I know, I know. Calm down."

Laura turned toward me, walking backward through the opening. "Rosemary. Find a way," she whispered.

"I promise!" We both ignored the way my voice cracked. My eyes were on Fenton's body as he reached the opening. "Wait!" I shouted, knowing I was being selfish.

Laura froze, her eyes wide with fear. "I just need to kiss him goodbye," I admitted, not even a little embarrassed. This was the last time I would get to see my soulmate for a very long time. Shoving the guard aside, I tugged the blanket apart and found the storybook prince I had fallen in love with, even without a beating heart.

I leaned in close. "I love you forever, Fenton Lynch," I whispered, then pressed my lips to his. I nearly gasped at the feel of him. Waxy and ice cold, like death. I pulled away, tears pricking my eyes. "Go, Laura! Hurry!"

She immediately began pulling him and I pushed his feet as long as I could. I clasped my folded hands to my chest, praying, wishing, begging for her to make it, for him to survive. The pleas fell from my mouth as they disappeared out of sight.

The guard shoved me back and I stumbled. I caught sight of a dozen more shadow-like figures coming toward me. I recognized quite a few of them from our fights on Earth. "Well, hello there, friends. Come to visit me?"

I took off at a dead run, back toward the cave. I needed to get to the portal in the pond. I had to get back to the world of the living to make sure Fenton made it out alive.

The pissed off demons flew overhead and gathered at the opening of the cave, blocking my exit. Well, that wasn't great. "Seriously? You're all still mad about a little fight?" I probably shouldn't taunt demons, but I was already dead and already in Hell. How much worse could it get?

I turned and started running back toward the other portal. It would be easier to take out one guard than a group of demons. I was nearly there when my steps faltered and I fell to a knee as a sharp pain blossomed in my chest, where my heart used to be. I gasped, my hands flying to my ribs, and doubled over in pain. My chest moved with the inhale of oxygen, and I sputtered, choking on the taste of sulfur and oxygen.

Underneath my hand, I felt the bass-drum beat of a pulse. Panicked, I looked at the guard. Another shadow, dark and shapeless, lifted off me, like steam from warm pavement after a rainstorm.

"The curse?" I gasped, my throat raw and aching. "How?"

His eyes, completely black and empty, watched me. "True love's kiss."

No. A true love's kiss would mean Fenton was dead. *Dead.*

"NO!" I screamed. I stood up on shaky legs, ignoring the group of demons who were following me, trying to suck the curse into themselves like cigarette smoke. I stumbled and fell again, skinning my knees and palms. I scrambled back to my feet and ran at the guard. "MOVE!" I ordered.

He didn't move fast enough, so I charged right into him and wrapped my arms around him. If he wasn't going to move, he could come with me. I screamed with fury as we fell through the veil.

We crashed onto the Pont d'Amor, landing so hard the pavement cracked. My head screamed with pain and I blinked hard, trying to clear my vision. My chest constricted until I gasped for air, the copper taste of blood stinging my mouth.

The guard hovered over me, pushing down on my windpipe. I kicked hard, dislodging him and rolling to the side, white-hot pain blinding me for a few seconds. A gunshot went off and the demon dissipated into smoke. I rolled my eyes upwards and saw Javier holding a rifle and running toward me.

Quick footfalls shook the bridge, or maybe it was just me shivering. I spit out the blood filling my mouth. Javier knelt down next to me and guided me to my back. I cried out as a wave of intolerable, searing pain turned my stomach inside out. Everything around me spun too fast and I closed my eyes.

I marveled for a moment at the overwhelming feeling of *feeling*. I had been numb for so long, every sensation was devastating. I missed the numbness right now.

My ears were ringing, but I could make out Javier's worried shouts as I watched him strip off his hoodie and ball it up, then used it to apply pressure to my stomach. I tried to look at what he was doing, but he gently pushed me back down.

Loren appeared by my side in only a t-shirt, a long-sleeved shirt was in his hand. He twisted it then wrapped it incredibly tight around my upper thigh and I moaned in discomfort. My chest burned with each breath, and when Loren ran his hand over my ribs, I gripped his wrist so hard, he winced. My body arched off the ground as the pain washed through me from hairline to toes. I had only felt this much pain the night I died.

The realization hit me like the car had; the curse was broken, and I was human again, but I was only as human as I was in the moments before I died. After all of that, I was still going to die from a car crash that happened three years ago.

I tugged on Loren's wrist. His dark eyes met mine and he leaned in close. "Fen...ton?" I breathed.

His gaze went to a group of people on the other side of the bridge and then back to me, eyes glassy. "He's alive," he whispered. "Grayson did CPR. He's breathing."

I nodded and smiled weakly. "Sis...take care...her..." I wheezed, the pain in my chest robbing me of words. I blinked, trying to stay conscious.

"You're going to have to tell her that yourself. So you better pull it together, Evanora. You're not dying on me," he said.

Even before I heard her scream, I knew Hazel saw me. Call it the "twin thing," but something strong and invisible wrapped itself around my heart.

I coughed, only stopping when she kneeled down near my head and pressed her forehead upside down against mine. Calmness flooded through me, and I sank into our bond. "I'm right here," she promised. "I'm right here, Romi. Stay with me a little longer, okay?"

I nodded, even though I knew a *little* longer was all I had. "Same...accident..."

She held the sides of my face. "I already watched you die once. I'm not letting you die on me again."

Flashing lights pulled up to the bridge. When the paramedic arrived and asked about the injuries, Hazel lifted her head and said, "Car accident...hit and run."

I closed my eyes, not wanting to listen anymore. I just needed a little rest. Fenton was okay and back where he belonged. He had survived Hell. My sister had forgiven me. The boys would take care of her.

With a shuddering breath, I let myself fall into the darkness.

16

Magic was powerful, and healing witches could do amazing things, but even they had limitations when dealing with the aftereffects of devil magic. Still hooked up to my own IV because of severe dehydration and heat stroke—I had lost nearly fifteen pounds in Hell, despite only being gone about four human hours—I wheeled to the room in intensive care and hovered in the doorway.

Romi was being kept sedated to allow her body to heal. She had major internal bleeding, a fractured pelvis, several broken bones, a punctured lung, and a long list of things they were concerned about. But after forty-eight hours, she was still alive, which was a good sign.

Hazel was asleep on Grayson's lap in a recliner. When they had argued family only, Grayson made a donation to the hospital and started calling Hazel his fiancée. At least, that's what Loren told me.

Loren's hand gripped my shoulder, as if reassuring both of us that we were still there, together. Grayson's eyes moved from the television to us, then very carefully, he slipped out from underneath Hazel and covered her in a fleece blanket Raine had dropped off earlier. Loren had used the fiancée line to get her in as well.

Grayson stood on the other side of me, hand on my other shoulder. Romi looked so small, so frail in the giant hospital bed. I wasn't ashamed of the tears that pooled in my eyes and rolled down my cheeks. My brothers each squeezed me tight and I knew all between us was forgiven.

"How'd you break the curse?" Loren asked quietly.

I shrugged. "I don't know, honestly. I remember being in Hell...and I remember Mom. She was there with Raine's mom..." I closed my eyes, missing Mom right then as much as I had the day she died. "Fuck."

I sucked in a steadying breath and brushed the back of my hand against my eyes roughly. "Anyway, my body just gave out. Then I woke up in the hospital."

Grayson cleared his throat, but his voice was still thick with emotion. "I saw Mom, the night we found you. I had dozed off on the couch and thought I was dreaming. She told me to get to the bridge."

Loren breathed in sharply through his nose. "Same. I thought I was going crazy until Raine admitted that she saw Genevieve. Raine got to say goodbye this time." He shifted his weight from one foot to the other. "Mom told me not to blame myself anymore."

I nodded. "Definitely stop doing that. You need to forgive yourself of a lot of shit before you die, because let me tell you, Hell is terrible."

"When you're feeling up to it, we should record everything you remember," Loren said.

"Tomorrow."

We all glanced at Hazel as she stirred but didn't wake.

I looked at Loren. "Did Galinda come by?"

"Yeah. She played a pretty convincing aunt. The purple eyes helped." Loren frowned and glanced at Grayson. "Did she give Hazel something to knock her out? I've never seen her that still."

Grayson nodded. "Yeah. She was making herself sick with worry and Galinda finally convinced her."

"Good." He ran a hand over his buzzed head. "The creams and potions can only do so much without a gray witch. Romi's got a long road ahead of her."

I covered my face with my hands. "What if..." I let my hands fall into my lap. My brothers were silent, but they didn't need to say anything. If something happened to her, they'd be there for me.

Grayson shoved a hand into my hair and kissed the top of my head. "Go rest. I'll come by in a bit."

They exchanged a half hug before Loren drove my wheelchair back to my room. "Do you ever wonder what life would be like if we fell for regular humans?" I asked.

He helped me to bed and covered me with blankets, and then sat down in a recliner before answering. "Nah." He kicked off his shoes and leaned back. "We were not made for boring lives, little bro."

17

FENTON

Three months later

I lifted Romi from the car and set her in a wheelchair, blindfolded. She laughed and tried to tug the blind-fold off.

"Nope. Leave that on or no surprise."

She gave me an adorable little huff and I leaned down to kiss the tip of her nose. "You know I'm able to walk a little bit."

I chuckled. "There's ice everywhere. This way you won't fall and break something."

Even with Galinda's help, Romi still needed to go through physical therapy for her injuries. We had stayed at Hazel and Grayson's new place, because it was only one level. While it was fun spending time with my brother and Hazel, I knew when Romi no longer needed constant care that the time had finally come to find our own space.

We couldn't sublet Hazel's apartment with so many

stairs, but with the help of a cash offer on a house and a work crew who responded well to bribes, our new ranch was officially ready a month and a half after I signed on the dotted line.

After pushing Romi's chair up the custom ramp I had added to the side of our new home, I fished the key out of my pocket. Inserting it into the lock, I paused. "You ready?"

I didn't have to see her eyes to know she rolled them. "No. Never. Let's just stay like this for three hours."

I stood very still. "I've been to Hell and back. I can stand here for three hours and not flinch." What started as a joke fell flat when she stiffened. "I'm sorry. Just...joking about it is sometimes the only way I can get through."

She reached back and touched my arm. "You're allowed to make Hell jokes. As long as we never have to go back."

I brought her hand up to my lips. "Deal." I unlocked the door, put the brakes on the chair, and hoisted Romi into my arms.

She laughed and wrapped her arms around my neck, and I stole a quick kiss. I paused a moment to appreciate everything that was *right* in this moment—something I had been doing since I left the hospital. The woman I loved was healing and was in my arms with her vanilla and mint scent dancing around me.

"What are you doing, weirdo?" She laughed as I sniffed her hair.

"Enjoying the little moments."

She snuggled into my neck. "I do that now, too."

I kissed her forehead, then reached out and opened the door. Walking through, I shut it with my foot. "Blindfold off."

Without wasting another moment, she pulled it off and looked around. Her mouth fell open as she took in what used to be a shrine to the seventies, which now looked like a high-end Parisian apartment. Everything was white but ornate. From the crown molding to the new bathroom door, to the built-in shelves.

It was the complete opposite of the darkness in Hell.

We were standing in a combined living and dining room, which led to a kitchen with a chef's stove and double oven. The doorways had been widened into gaping archways, making the home not only seem more open but easier to navigate with a wheelchair. I knew Romi wasn't going to be in one for her entire life, but I hadn't wanted her to struggle at home for a single day.

The newly refinished blond, hardwood floors shone in the sunlight that glittered through the new, insulated windows. Thick, deep purple curtains were tied back, the pop of color in an otherwise pastel room.

She spotted the dog bed in the corner and looked up at me. "We have a dog?"

I smiled and kissed her nose. "There's one named Lenny I'd like to bring home if you're okay with it?"

She nodded enthusiastically. "Let's go get him right now!"

I laughed and readjusted her in my arms. "Slow down, tiger. We'll go tomorrow. Let me show you my favorite room." She giggled as I walked us to the master bedroom. It was painted with a blue so light, it was nearly white.

A chandelier hung from stylish exposed beams and illuminated the king-size bed with a tall headboard. Romi put her legs on the ground and slipped out of my arms, then slowly turned in a circle. Her eyes were wet, and her mouth was hanging open, but she still hadn't spoken. She slowly moved to a giant charcoal canvas of Notre Dame that hung on the wall. She touched the edge, and I didn't miss that her fingers were shaking.

Hurrying to her side, I wrapped my arms around her waist and gently kissed her neck. "Say something," I said quietly. I could barely hear the words over my pounding heart.

"I can't find any words. It's like...you saw inside my head." She put her arms on top of mine. "I love you, you know."

I pulled her tighter against me. "*Je t'aime, mon ange.*"

She turned to face me and pushed an errant curl back from my forehead.

I leaned down and pressed my lips to hers, still marveling in their softness, in their warmth. I swear, I could feel the moment her soul touched mine each time I kissed her. It was like us being dead, together, made us inseparable.

Once she had gotten out of the hospital, Romi told me how I had basically died before Mom had pulled me through the portal. Our goodbye kiss had broken the curse and probably saved us both. Her kisses still felt like life, even now.

I pulled away but kept my face close. "So, Grayson and Hazel are packing our stuff as we speak. You ready to move in?"

She squealed and hugged me so tight, I was afraid she'd break her arms.

She let her hands fall lower on my back and then slipped them into the back pockets of my jeans. I was aware of every inch of the pressure of her hands. "Now that we're alone and both healed—"

I raised an eyebrow.

She laughed lightly. "Alright, mostly healed, I'd like to

make use of that bed later." Her cheeks went bright red, but her gaze held mine.

My heart thumped hard, once. "Are you sure you're ready?"

"We just need to be careful with my hip. But, we'll finally be alone. In our new place."

I nipped at her bottom lip. "Let's get settled and then we'll see how you feel, okay?"

She stepped back but held on to my arms for support. "Fenton, just because I'm still working through my injuries, doesn't mean I'm incapable of making love with you."

My heart beat a little faster, but with anxiety instead of arousal. She didn't remember how she screamed when the morphine wore off, at how she cried because the sheets abraded her oversensitive new skin, or the endless tubes and needles. She didn't know how it felt sitting by the edge of her bed praying that she didn't have brain damage.

The first few weeks after she had returned to her human body had all been lost in a haze of narcotics and pain, or at least that was what she told me. Eventually, her body started working with her instead of against her. She got used to the feeling of hot and cold, fabric and touch. Her lungs remembered how to fill with air and her pain, although constant, had been reduced to a tolerable level.

As she snuggled into my arms each night, I wanted to kiss her until she was shaking, until we became one. But with each kiss and each caress, I heard her screams in my memory. I couldn't risk hurting her again, even if the doctor said she was cleared for physical activity.

She pulled away from me and sat down on the bed, her exhaustion evident in her purple eyes. They had changed from blue sometime between her appearing on the bridge and waking up in the hospital. Although she wasn't practicing much of her craft yet, I knew she was eager to relearn the basics.

"Let me nap," she yawned. "Then we can officially move in and have that serious discussion I see brewing behind your eyes."

I helped her into the brand new bed, and she snuggled deeper between the blankets. I kissed her cheek, then silently left the room. After pulling her wheelchair inside and placing it in the hallway outside of the bedroom, so she could reach it easily, I went out the front door and sat on the steps.

The February wind was brutal, but I didn't mind. My stinging cheeks reminded me that I was still alive. Since we had returned from Hell, everything had felt like it was on hold. My focus had been on Romi getting better and finding a place to start our lives together.

Now that we had time to slow down and enjoy life, I didn't know how to stop being scared. This had been the hardest three months of my life, from facing my own fears in Hell, to almost losing my soulmate. I wouldn't even do more than kiss her, for fear that I'd hurt her.

I pulled my knit cap down tighter and left my gloved hands on the back of my head, trying to slow down my racing thoughts. The crunch of tires on packed snow made me jerk upright, and I saw Loren's truck pull into the driveway. He jumped out and walked over, hands deep in his pockets. "She resting?" he asked.

I moved over and he sat down on the step next to me. "Yeah."

"She like it?"

I nodded. "Loved it."

He elbowed me. "You freaking out?"

I nodded again.

He sighed and then lifted his head to scan the trees separating us from the road. "I haven't been to Hell, but I've seen some shit." He looked down on his boots, as if waiting for them to say something. "It's...hard to get past it. To believe that something good can actually happen. To trust that the woman you love is really safe and healthy and not going to disappear like everything else."

After letting his words hover in the air for a long moment, he turned to face me, holding my gaze with his. "You've had a few really terrible years—I mean we all have —but these last four months have been even worse. Being kidnapped, literally going to Hell, and nearly losing Romi."

He grabbed my knee. "But don't forget, you reunited with Gray and me, and we're not going anywhere. You're home, okay? It's time to hang your hat and just accept it's going to be okay."

I wiped a hand roughly down my face, my nose already so numb I barely felt the pressure. "I'm so afraid I'm going to do something that will hurt her."

"You've got to trust her. She'll tell you her limits. All you need to do is listen." He reached into his back pocket and pulled out his wallet, then procured a business card to give to me. "That's my therapist. She specializes in...strange situations."

I took it from him and read the simple black type on the white face. "Like escaping from Hell?"

"Like escaping from Hell." He tucked his wallet back in his pocket. "I do video chat appointments. I think it may be good for you to talk to someone."

I put the card in my coat pocket. "I will, thanks."

Loren squeezed my knee then stood up. "Well, my ass is frozen. I'll see you for dinner tonight."

I got to my feet and gave him a quick hug, then stepped back, confused. "Hey, why'd you come by?"

He shrugged. "Knew you probably needed your favorite brother today." He waved then climbed into his truck and drove away.

I fingered the card in my pocket as I walked back into the house. *Trust her. She'll tell you her limits.* Maybe it was time I listened to my big brother's advice.

18

ROMI

Pain was exhausting and needing to sleep so often when I hadn't needed sleep in years was disconcerting. Sleep reminded me of dying, and for the first few weeks, I was terrified that I'd never wake up. With Fenton holding me at night, however, I've learned to just stay in the moment and appreciate every minute that I have to be alive again. Well, that and the new anti-anxiety medication my doctor had put me on.

Despite the panic attacks, I loved everything about being alive—truly alive—again. Even when I needed help getting out of bed and taking a shower. Although, I did really miss kicking the shit out of demons, which was something I needed to talk to Loren about when I was back on my feet.

As the early winter night chased the sun away, a knock at the door revealed my twin sister. I waved and pushed myself up, brushing the hair out of my face. "I'm awake," I croaked.

She climbed onto the bed and put her head next to mine on the pillow. "How you feeling?"

I held up a hand and gave her the "so-so" gesture. "I

think the cold makes me sore." She nodded. The windchill today was no joke. "But, I'm better every day."

She reached over to Fenton's nightstand and flipped on a lamp, then turned back to smile at me. "Come on, we're having a dinner party. Fenton's been waiting to cook until you were awake. Grayson and Loren are unloading the stuff you had at our place. And I have some makeup to do on you."

I yawned then rolled to my back. "Why are we doing my makeup?"

She gave me a one-armed shrug. "One, because makeup always makes me feel better. Two, because you probably want to get lucky tonight."

I gave her my best shocked face and pinched her under her arm. She poked me in the ribs. "Tell me it's a lie!" she said on a laugh. "You're alone for the first time in your own home, you're both alive, you're feeling better..."

I rolled my eyes dramatically. "It's not a lie. I just..." I put my hands up in a shrug. "I died before I had the chance to have sex. It's kind of a big deal. And Fenton doesn't really seem like he's ready for it."

She brushed her hand through my hair and pushed it back from my face. "Why do you think he's waiting?"

I stared at the ceiling for a long moment. "I think he's afraid he'll hurt me."

"Will he?"

I shrugged again. "I don't know. Maybe. But I'm willing to try."

She sat up and scooted off the bed. "Well, come on Sleeping Beauty. Let's get some eyeliner on and deal with that hair. If you're going to have sex for the first time tonight, you're going to feel like a fucking princess. And we need to get the awkward sex talk out of the way, too."

I laughed as she walked around the bed and helped me stand, my body fighting against the movement. We made it to my chair, and she pushed me into the hallway calling, "We're awake! Cook away!"

Fenton called back a thank you and the sound of a kitchen coming to life made the house feel like home. We rolled into the bathroom and Hazel got to work with her curling iron, giving me beachy waves in the middle of winter. When she was done with the left side of my hair, she put the curling iron down. "Listen," she said. "We need to talk about sex."

I looked up at her. "We do?"

She nodded. "I know that this is your first time with someone and while I don't subscribe to this virginity is special bullshit, I want to make sure you know that you and Fenton can and should talk to each other about your expectations, wants, and needs. If you can't talk about sex, you shouldn't be having it."

The tops of my ears went hot, but I held her gaze. "Thanks, sis."

"It's always a choice, every time, for both of you. Okay? And you have to respect his decision if he's not ready yet. He went through Hell, too—literally and figuratively."

She fussed with a curl. "I'm going to put condoms in your nightstand."

"Thank you." I reached up and grabbed her forearm. "I'll talk to him, promise."

She searched my face for a moment and then picked up the iron and got back to work on my hair. "And if he even looks at you wrong, I will make him ooze puss from every orifice."

I laughed so hard I snorted. "I'll make sure to tell him that."

Raine came in with wine glasses full of pink liquid. She ran her eyes from my head to my feet, presumably checking that I was still hale and whole, before handing me a glass. "It's carbonated fruit juice. You shouldn't mix alcohol and medication."

I toasted her and Hazel and took a big whiff of the fruity beverage before I tasted it. "The carbonation really brings out the grape juice taste," I teased.

Hazel swirled it around in her glass. "It has good legs."

Raine sipped and made a thinking face. "Definitely made from the finest grapes in Michigan."

We laughed and drank pure sugar while Hazel and Raine talked about the remodel at Billy's Blues and BBQ. They were hoping to reopen by spring. After Hazel finished my makeup and moved on to Raine's, Tiffany stuck her head in. "Can I squeeze in, too?"

"Yes!" I promised. The bathroom, while nearly too skinny for my chair, was long, with a double vanity and two mirrors. Raine sat on the counter while Hazel worked on her face, leaving the edge of the tub open for Tiffany.

"So, haven't seen you in awhile," I said. I smirked when her cheeks turned red. "I knew it!"

Hazel and Raine looked between us. "Knew what?" Hazel asked.

I finished the rest of my grape juice and set the glass on the edge of the tub. "I know I'm not dead anymore, but I'm still fairly perceptive." I winked. "That and she's got a hickey peeking out from the edge of her scarf."

Hazel gasped and Raine's mouth fell open. "Who?" Raine asked, reaching over and pulling down the scarf. Tiffany swatted her away.

A bark of male laughter trailed in from the living room. Laughter from a man I thought had left town a few months ago. "It seems that someone brought a date to dinner," I teased. "How long has Javier been in town?"

She covered her face in her hands as Hazel and Raine jumped and screamed like we were in a high school movie. Hazel then ran to the door, opened it up and yelled, "Hi Javier! *¿Cómo estás?*"

"*Muy bien,* Hazel. *¿E tu?*" he called back.

She giggled and Tiffany jumped off the counter and tried to push the door closed. "I'm *muy bien*, too, Javier!" she said before letting the door close.

I threw my head back and laughed so loud, everyone turned to look at me. Hazel tilted her head, a silent question. "It's so special to be here with the three of you instead of just haunting random places around town." I should've probably expected the group hug that followed my statement but it still took me by surprise. As did the joy at being able to feel my sister and my friends.

THE EVENING WAS like one of those made-for-television movies. Fenton had outdone himself with dinner, then we cleaned up and played silly card games until nearly ten. Javier held Tiffany's hand most of the night and when she hugged me goodbye, she promised to call me tomorrow with all the details.

Hazel and Raine had unpacked what few things I had collected since becoming human, with a promise that they could take me shopping next week. Then, finally, it was just Fenton and me.

He helped me onto the couch and wrapped his arms around me, pulling me onto his lap, my back to his chest. "Did you have a good evening?"

My face ached from so much smiling. "It was the absolute best."

"Welcome home," he said softly and kissed me on the neck near my shoulder, then squeezed me even tighter. His body heat seeped through my long sleeve shirt and warmed my skin.

"Wherever you are is home," I admitted.

He responded with another kiss on my neck, his lips sending a wave of heat spiking through me. I reached back and sank my hands into his hair, pulling him back down to my exposed skin. He followed my lead and continued kissing the sensitive area, chasing the breath from my body and curling my toes. I tilted my head to the side to give him more access.

I could feel him harden beneath me and I leaned into him, needing more. "Fen, take me to bed," I whispered. "Please."

Breathing hard, as if he had run a marathon, he leaned his head against mine. "Are you sure?"

I nodded. "I've never been more sure."

He paused for a few moments. "Did an STI test while I was in the hospital and everything was negative." His hands skated down my sides and over my thighs and the air in the room grew so thick, I could barely breathe.

It took me a few tries to remember how to speak when he pressed up into me. "Hazel said she put some condoms in my nightstand," I admitted. "I just started the pill this month, so we need to use backup."

"Are you sure you're ready?" he asked against my skin.

I shifted a little so I could look at him over my shoulder. "I have been ready since the day I first saw you."

His smile lit up the room. "Same, Rosemary Evanora. Same." In one fluid motion, he swept me off the couch and walked us down the hall to our bedroom. He gently deposited me onto the mattress before he took off his shirt and jeans, leaving his boxers on.

I caught a glimpse of the small but complicated cross tattoo—the symbol of the witch hunter—on his shoulder blade. Normally that marking, made with ink that had been magically treated to repel witches, would burn my skin at mere contact, but his mark never bothered me. I wasn't sure if it was his pacifist ways or the fact that we were in love, but I was glad not to have another thing standing between us.

As he crawled toward me, I tried not to look at the scars on his neck from the bite marks the hellhound left behind. It was a physical reminder of what he had been through because of me, and I knew it was going to be a long time before I came to terms with that. Tonight, we were going to continue the journey toward healing.

I lifted my arms, indicating that he should take off my shirt. He complied, then pulled my mouth to his, sucking on my bottom lip. I would never get sick of his kisses. I would walk through Hell again for a hundred years to feel them just once.

"Promise to tell me if anything hurts or it's too much?" he asked.

I held the side of his head and waited until his gaze focused on mine. "Yes. Now stop talking and make love to me, Fenton Lynch!"

With a laugh, he carefully leaned me back and pulled off my jeans, followed by my underwear and bra. He stood there, staring at me like he hadn't helped me shower and change countless times. "You are so beautiful," he breathed. "Inside and out."

I bit my lip, heat coursing through me. "Ditto," I teased.

With a smile, he bent down and kissed my ankle, then

up my calf. His tongue darted out and slipped around the back of my knee, making me giggle. He was gentle as he traced the pink, puckered scar on my thigh and the surgery scar on my hip. His mouth trailed across my stomach and down my other leg, until I was dizzy with anticipation.

My chest was heaving like I had just run a marathon and I clutched the sheets as he carefully spread my legs wider, watching my face for any pain, and kissed the inside of my thighs, then higher. If I would walk through Hell for a hundred years for his kisses, I would walk a thousand years to relive the first moment he captured me in his mouth.

My hands dug into his hair as he made love to me with his tongue, savoring and caressing me, teasing and stroking. So many feelings I had never felt—even when I had solo sessions as a fumbling teen—clogged my chest and filled my throat. His eyes met mine as he slid one finger inside of me. I gasped at the burning sensation and my hip tensed in a new way that made me flinch. He immediately stilled and waited until I had adjusted the position of my leg.

"I'm okay," I promised. "Don't stop."

With a wicked smile, he started moving again, and warmth gathered low in my body, twisting and tightening. He carefully added a second finger and I cried out, but in pleasure this time. Every part of my body was overwhelmed by sensation, and I was getting closer and closer to falling over the edge.

It was one simple kiss, a steady push inside, and I burst apart. His free hand helped guide my leg so I wouldn't hurt myself as my entire body tensed and released, like the last bolt of a thunderstorm. He pulled out of me and crawled over my body as I came back down to Earth.

I kissed him softly and then deeper as he stroked my

head, my neck, my chest. His hands cupped my breasts, his thumbs circling my nipples, relighting the fire he had just turned to smoke. "We don't have to go any further tonight," he said, his voice rough, as if the words rolled over sandpaper.

"I want all of you." I met his eyes, then let my hand trace down his body, past the dusting of hair at his chest, and to the darker hair between his legs.

He let me play for only a few strokes before he pulled me away. "Let's revisit that later. I want to be inside of you." His blue eyes looked like fire as he kissed me roughly and thoroughly, a promise of what was to come. He pulled away and yanked open my nightstand, grabbing a condom and rolling it on.

"How are we going to do this?" I asked, kissing him again. I couldn't bear his weight on me just yet.

Fenton laid down on his side. "Lay on your good side, back facing me."

I nodded and turned myself over. He grabbed one of his pillows and put it between my knees. His fingers made soothing movements along my sore hip, making my skin tingle.

"Does anything hurt?"

I shook my head. "Now shut up and make love to me."

He laughed softly. "Please embroider that on something for me."

I twisted my head and kissed his nose. "I promise."

He pulled my back tight against his chest. "I love you, Rosemary. I'm yours until the end of time. Heaven, Hell, here, I don't care."

I blinked away the sting in my eyes. "You jump, I jump." He leaned over, tilted my face toward him, and kissed me hard. "*Je t'aime*," I whispered against his lips.

He shifted us carefully, then positioned himself at my entrance. "If anything hurts too bad, or your hip—"

"If you don't stop talking, I will consider smothering you with a pillow."

He laughed and put his forehead against the back of my neck. Then he pushed in slowly.

I gasped at the intrusion, gripping his forearms at the sensation. "I'm okay," I promised, focusing on relaxing my muscles.

A harsh breath escaped his lips as he tried to reposition himself at a better angle without putting pressure on my hip. We worked together through the burning sensation until he completely filled me. One arm clamped tightly around my waist while the other dug into my hair and I closed my eyes. I was in Heaven.

He moved us slowly, carefully, keeping me as still as possible as he thrust in and out, dragging each stroke with precision.

When he was sure I could handle more, he went faster then faster still, his mouth kissing every single inch of skin he could reach. My lower back was starting to burn, and I shifted a little to relieve the pressure. "Back is starting to hurt, but don't you dare stop," I managed, even as he drove into me again and a spike of pleasure nearly stole my breath.

He slipped a hand between us and began rhythmically rubbing my clit until every muscle grew taught and released like a hundred fireworks, like thunder. A sob escaped me as he made the sexiest groan I had ever heard and pulsed inside of me.

I didn't bother to hide my tears as he laid me down, then removed the condom. He immediately began massaging my hips and legs. "Why are you crying?" he asked quietly, helping me push into a stretch I had learned in physical therapy.

I smiled as he tried to wipe my face with the sheet. "Because I have never felt anything like that."

He smiled. "Yeah?"

I nodded. "Yeah. You're stuck with me, Lynch."

"I'm not mad at that."

After helping me clean up and get ready for bed, we snuggled naked under the thick blankets. He wrapped his arms around me and sighed in contentment. Then he started laughing.

"What?" I asked on a yawn.

"Rosemary Evanora. Are you trying to levitate right now?"

I frowned. "I...what?" He loosened his hold and my body started to rise off the bed. I groaned and put my hands over my face. "I mean, I knew it was a thing, but I kind of forgot about it. Yeah, I'm floating. It's temporary."

He threw his head back and laughed, the sound squeezing around my heart. "How do you know it's a thing?"

"It happened to Hazel after she and Grayson..." I didn't really want to talk about my sister's sex life while I was naked. "Anyway, it's a soulmate thing. When witches find their soulmate, they float."

He draped his leg carefully over my knees to keep me on the bed and kissed my nose. "Soulmate, huh?"

I shrugged. "Knew that the instant I saw you."

I felt his smile against my lips. "How's that?"

"It's a ghost thing," I teased.

He kissed me, soft and sweet. We held each other, nose to nose in the dark. I tried to take a mental snapshot of this moment.

"Rosemary?"

"Yeah?"

"What's next for our life adventure?" His fingers continued to stroke my body, leaving goosebumps chasing his touch.

"Well," I kissed him. "We're going to do that a lot. Like way more times."

He chuckled. "Agreed."

"Then, I'm going to talk to Loren about helping him locate demons." He tensed under me and I ran my fingers over the nape of his neck to relax him. "Don't worry, only locating. Not fighting. Okay?"

He growled. "We'll talk more about that when I don't have sleepy sex brain."

"Sleepy sex brain, huh?"

"It's like being drunk, but way better."

I laughed. "I agree." I kissed his forehead. "I think I want to go to school to be a French teacher. Then, I want to get married, go to Paris for our honeymoon, then maybe have a few kids. Adopt a few more."

He pulled me closer to him. "You say the word and I'm in."

"What about you?" I tucked an errant curl behind his ear.

He took a deep breath. "Just want to be near my family and be with you. Love cooking." He sighed. "Your plan sounds like a great life. Let's do that."

"It's the best. Because we're together."

His lips savored mine for a long moment. "Always, Rosemary. Always."

EPILOGUE

HAZEL

Halloween, later that year

With a smile, I turned on the generator Grayson and Loren had set up on the end of the bridge. Romi squealed and clapped her hands as Raine and I high-fived. This year's Halloween decorations went above and beyond what we had done before.

Thousands of orange and purple twinkle lights hung from trees, fake ghosts were suspended from branches, life-sized witches and monster dolls wearing the Billy's Blues and BBQ uniforms sat on the edge of the bridge, holding candy and popcorn. Surround sound blasted all my favorite Halloween tunes and propane heaters lined the side of the bridge so the crowd would not freeze in the early winter weather.

Everything was perfect.

My favorite police officer, Jimmy, walked over from his car, then stood next to me with his arms folded. "So…"

"So." I bumped his shoulder. "Ready for tonight?"

He sighed. "I don't really have a choice, do I?"

"Don't worry. Pretty much everyone here is a regular human." After we had told Jimmy about the Other side of Hayvenwood, it took him awhile to get used to the idea, and even longer before he could look me in the eye. But he was finally back to his old self. Mostly.

"I'm not worried. You're the one who's most likely to cause trouble," he teased, giving me a wink.

I laughed. "Truer words were never spoken."

He tilted his head to the large tables set up on either end of the bridge. "Food ready?"

I gestured for him to head to Billy's table, which was laden with food and desserts Fenton had spent two days making. "Be my guest."

Tiffany and Javier—who had become inseparable when he wasn't on a mission—volunteered to serve food tonight, meaning that I just had to stand there in my witch hat and Billy's uniform looking pretty. My favorite kind of night off. Since expanding and reopening the restaurant, local bands had been coming in every week, making us a popular spot for not only Hayvenwood, but the entire area. It was hard and grueling work, and I wouldn't change a single second.

Fenton's recipes, Raine's piano playing and connections in the music industry, Loren's gift with numbers, and Grayson's ability to do almost any job he was asked—although, we never asked him to serve food again—really made the place a family restaurant. Also, having my sister as a part-time bartender was pretty great, too.

She was also a newly enrolled Hayvenwood University freshman and out of the wheelchair on most days, unless the pain flared up. I watched as she walked over to me, no longer limping. My heart swelled—but I'd never tell anyone that. It'd ruin my street cred. "What's up, Rom?"

"It's way awesomer being a human at this shindig," she said, shoving a mini-candy bar into her mouth. "You know, except for the getting cold thing."

I hugged my sister, rubbing her arms. "That's why I told you to wear long underwear."

She buried her glacier-like nose against the bit of my neck that was exposed around my scarf, making me squeak. "I wore two pairs!" she defended.

Laughing, Fenton came over and draped his coat over her shoulders. "Come on, ice cube. Let's go stand by a heater before you give Hazel frostbite."

"Why is her nose always so cold?" I asked him.

"It's like the tundra," he agreed.

Romi rolled her eyes. "Yeah, yeah."

The bridge soon filled up with college kids and locals who couldn't say no to free samples and candy. On this bridge, you were never too old to Trick or Treat. Grayson and I handed out flyers for our upcoming concerts and gave away handfuls of candy. By nine-thirty, even my nose was completely numb and my feet were on fire, and I was having the time of my life.

During a lull, I put my freezing face against Grayson's neck, causing him to swear, and then pull me close against him. "How are you this cold? Can you magic up some heat forcefield or something?"

I pulled back and raised an eyebrow. "That's not exactly how healing magic works, you know."

He grumbled, "It should be," as I returned my face to his skin.

Romi appeared next to me. "Want me to try and conjure up a personal heater or something?" she asked. She had started to go through Grandma's books to try her hand at some simple spells but was staying far away from dark magic.

"Nah," I replied. "I've got this guy. He's all I need."

Neither of them responded and when I lifted my head, I caught Grayson and Romi having a silent conversation. Then, my sister made a motion with her hand and the music cut off. A sultry voice came over the sound system and I turned to find Raine attaching a mic to a stand next to her keyboard near the Billy's table.

"This is a special request tonight from our not-so-new guy, Grayson." The familiar chords followed, the same crooner classic that Raine played the first time I danced with my boyfriend.

I looked up and him and shook my head, a huge smile on my face. "You're an idiot."

"You mispronounced romantic." He grasped my hand in his and started swaying. "Dance with me."

"It appears I have no choice." I gave him a quick kiss. "But yes, I will."

He spun me around, eliciting a few hoots—most likely from Romi and Tiffany—and then brought his lips to my ear. "The last year with you has been the best year of my life, except for when I was six and got to sleep in a car bed."

Something warm and melty filled my chest and I bit my lip. "Same," I whispered back. "Except I had a princess canopy bed."

He chuckled and gave me a soft kiss, then pulled me even tighter against him. "Hazel, I have something I need to ask you."

"What's that?"

He gave me a quick kiss just beneath my ear then pulled away and dropped to one knee. I gasped, a kaleidoscope of butterflies filling my stomach. He pulled a plastic pumpkin from the inside pocket of his coat and opened the lid to reveal a beautiful black diamond band. My heart started running around my chest and I put my hand there to calm it.

He smiled my favorite, wicked smile and looked straight into my eyes. "I knew the first time you told me to 'fuck off' that you were it for me. I'll give you the not-safe-for-work speech later, but for now, surrounded by our made-family, our dear friends, and several hundred strangers, I have to tell you that I love you until the end of time. Marry me?"

The cacophony around us faded into the background as I stared into the gray eyes that had been my home for the last year. "Abso-fucking-lutely," I shouted. He stood and grabbed my waist, spinning me around and kissing me hard.

I heard Romi screaming and my smile grew to the point of pain. "I can't believe you just did that," I admitted when he set me down, but kept me in his arms. "And you kneeled in your new jeans. This really must be love."

He winked at me. "I've gotta keep you on your toes, future Mrs. Evanora-Lynch. You ready for our next adventure?"

I raised my eyebrow. "I didn't say I was going to take your last name."

He shrugged. "Whatever. As long as you stay with me."

I smiled so wide my eyes watered. Yeah...they totally watered because of my smile. That's the story I was going with. "Who knew a witch and a witch hunter would end up living Happily Ever After?"

"I did," he said against my mouth, before kissing me again.

So did I...and maybe it was time to thank the Pont d'Amor.

THANK YOU GIFT

Thank you for visiting Hayvenwood! Don't miss jumping into Grenadine for your next adventure. I'll give you the prequel from my multi-award-winning romantic comedy series *Luke Before Edie* just for signing up for my newsletter.

Sign up at: BookHip.com/VQCAJL

ACKNOWLEDGMENTS

I can't believe this book is finished! I loved hanging out in Hayvenwood. It feels like a lifetime has passed since I found these characters wandering around in the dark corner of my brain. For those of you with me from the beginning—I love and appreciate you!

The problem with taking four years to finish a book, is that I'd forgotten everyone I need to thank, but I'm going to do my best!

To you readers, especially my Tacotastic reader group, for your patience and understanding.

Lindee Robinson and my model Jeanette Fredricks—I'll never forget getting snowed in at our photoshoot. It was, although *terrifying*, some of the most fun I ever had. This cover will always make me smile. (Shout out to my little bro Matt who kept us entertained all evening!)

To my sister who heard me rant about this book for years, read multiple versions, and still got me birthday gifts. That's love.

To my editors and alpha/beta readers Janna Bonikowski, Elyssa Man, Ellie from My Brother's Editor, Rosa Sharon from iScream Proofreading Services, Amber Young, Erika Cooper, and Michelle Lux. *Merci beaucoup* and *gracias* to my French and Spanish speaking friends who helped me with translations!

To my dad and non-evil stepmom, love you! Thanks for not leaving me on the side of the road as a teenager.

Christina, Erin, Meika, Liz, Dana, all my GDRWA friends, and to everyone else who has taken the time to reach out to me, to offer advice, brainstorming, writing sprints, and a shoulder to cry on. I couldn't have done this without you. Thanks for believing in me even when I would rather eat my feelings and watch Netflix. (Special shout out to Matt, Lucie, and Misty for being so supportive!)

Finally, to Mr. Heather, who is the Fenton to my Romi.

Wishing You Laughter & Good Books,
    Heather

ABOUT THE AUTHOR

Bold, Breathtaking, Badass Romance.

When she's not pretending to be a rock star with purple hair, award-winning author Heather Novak is crafting sex positive romance novels to make you swoon! After her rare disease tried to kill her, Heather mutated into a superhero whose greatest power is writing stories that you can't put down.

Heather tries to save the world (like her late mama taught her) from her home in the coolest city in the world, Detroit, Michigan, where she lives with Mr. Heather and their hypoallergenic pets.

Follow her at www.HeatherNovak.Net

You can learn more about Heather's rare disease at: www. Hypopara.org